RETURN TO

Augie Hobble

LANE SMITH

ROARING BROOK PRESS • NEW YORK

Published by Roaring Brook Press
Roaring Brook Press is a division of Holtzbrinck Publishing Holdings Limited Partnership
175 Fifth Avenue, New York, New York 10010
mackids.com

Library of Congress Cataloging-in-Publication Data

Smith, Lane.
Return to Augie Hobble / Lane Smith. — First edition.
pages cm
Summary: New Mexico middle-schooler Augie Hobble grapples with adolescence, paranormal mysteries, an overdue Creative Arts project, and heartbreaking loss while working his father's theme park, Fairy Tale Place.
ISBN 978-1-62672-054-1 (hardback) — ISBN 978-1-62672-055-8 (ebook)
[1. Amusement parks—Fiction. 2. Best friends—Fiction. 3. Friendship—Fiction. 4. Bullies—Fiction. 5. Supernatural—Fiction. 6. Death—Fiction. 7. Family life—New Mexico—Fiction. 8. New Mexico—Fiction.] I. Title.
PZ7.S6538Ret 2015
[Fic]—dc23
2014033004

Roaring Brook Press books may be purchased for business or promotional use. For information on bulk purchases please contact Macmillan Corporate and Premium Sales Department at (800) 221-7945 x5442 or by email at specialmarkets@macmillan.com.

First edition 2015
Book design by Molly Leach
Printed in the United States of America by R. R. Donnelley & Sons Company; Harrisonburg, Virginia
10 9 8 7 6 5 4 3 2 1

For Jim Alexander

ONE

TAKING A BREAK behind Grandma's House I run into Moze Gooch. He's got his head off and he's smoking. He knows he's not supposed to smoke in the suit. It gets in the fur and makes it stink worse than usual.

"You're not supposed to smoke in the suit," I say.

"My, what a big mouth you have," he says.

"No, really," I say pointing to the cigarette.

He takes a drag. "My, what big eyes you have," he says. He thinks this is funny on account of he's playing the Big Bad Wolf. I've heard him use these lines before. I want to say something clever but he'd easily beat the clever out of me. He's older than me and big. His nose is crooked. His left ear looks like my cousin Ida's scrunchie.

"Shove off or I'll huff and puff..." He takes a deep breath like he's going to blow someone's house down but the smoke catches in his throat and he just spazzes out coughing. Idiot.

He checks his watch then puts his wolf head back on. He glares at me. Five seconds. Ten. His painted-on mouth is laughing but I can guarantee you he is not laughing behind there. Fifteen seconds. The last of the cigarette smoke escapes through the vent holes in his cartoon eyes. I snap his picture, then run as he chases me into the park.

The Park: Fairy Tale Place. Built in 1967. Bypassed since 2009. That's when the new water park with the Aqua Loop opened off Route 8. We're no longer what you call a destination spot, but we still get some locals, grown-ups who were tortured here as kids and now have kids of their own to torture.

But I'm the one being tortured today. About a million degrees on the thermometer and I'm sweating like a pig. A real pig, not a smiley concrete pig like at the straw, stick, and brick houses over on Pork Avenue. Most days I do custodial work, sweeping up ticket stubs and popcorn, but today Dad's got me painting the toadstools, polka-dotted

carved toads with seats on their heads. There's like a hundred dots on each one and I have to touch up all of them. I told Dad if he wanted to punish me with extra work I would drive the Storybook Train or helm the Jolly Roger Boat. Dad's just being ornery for some reason.

Okay, there *was* this:

Dear Mr. and Mrs. Hobble,

I regret to inform you that Augie has failed his Creative Arts final project. He may however redo his project for a remake grade, a course of action I strongly recommend.
IDEAS due: July 1
FINAL due: August 28

Much luck, much inspiration,
—Mr. Tindall

R. L. Tindall
Creative Arts, Room 12-B
Gerald R. Ford Middle School

"Creativity is contagious, pass it on" —ALBERT EINSTEIN

Who fails Creative Arts?

That was exactly what Mom was wondering last night.

"Who fails Creative Arts?" she said.

"I know. It was stupid," I said.

"What did the other kids do for their projects? What did Britt do?"

"Britt made a self-portrait with papier mâché that, if I have to be totally honest, looked more monkey than Britt."

"So, you go to summer school?" said Dad. "I was really counting on you to help out around the park." By "help out" he meant help him. He's the manager of Fairy Tale Place.

"No, I just need to make up the one project. I can still work at the park."

"Well, you better make it a good one," said Mom. "No Elmer's glue and macaroni."

"No Mom."

"Nothing with Popsicle sticks."

"No Mom."

Later in my bedroom I tossed the Popsicle sticks I was going to use on my project into the trash and took out a blank notebook.

I sharpened a pencil.

I opened the book to page one.

I sharpened another pencil.

I closed the book.

The cover said RETURN TO with blank lines for a name and address. I wrote in my name, AUGIE HOBBLE, and my address.

I opened the book again.

I stared at the blank page.

I closed the book.

I watched cat videos on YouTube.

TWO

FAIRY TALE PLACE is made up of four lands: Storybook Village, Birthday Town, Fort Fortitude, and the North Pole. It's decorated with lots of stripes and polka dots and molding called dentil because it looks like teeth. But most of our dentil is missing or crooked like the plastic gag teeth people wear on Halloween.

FORT FORTITUDE
PHOTO SPOT
Santa
124878
BAR
Star Trak
ADMIT ONE
424877
TICKET
25c
TO WIN
FAIRY TALE PLACE
PARKING LOT
ADMIT ONE
124872

ZOO
NorthPole
NEMO
Birthday Town
FTP
Main Gate
Rental of LOCKER
30
026177
story
Charley's
NO REFUND
FAIRY TALE PLACE
Vehicle PASS
$3.00
339132
DISPLAY ON DASH
Peanuts
ROUTE
66

We have seventy-eight workers, which is not enough. There's always something going wrong or breaking down. That's why I help out and why I have to know the rules. What are the rules? These are the rules.

RULE #1 We are HOSTS not employees.

RULE #2 The visitors are GUESTS not customers.

RULE #3 When the HOSTS are in the park they are ON STAGE and must remain IN CHARACTER for the GUESTS.

Dad says the worst thing a host can do is BREAK THE ILLUSION we are creating for the guests. So even though I'm not a costumed character when I walk ON STAGE I'm still a part of the show. If Santa says, "Ho, ho, ho, Augie, there's fresh cocoa in Mrs. Claus's kitchen," I don't say, "We're in the desert. It's a kajillion degrees in the shade." What I say is, "Marshmallows too?" If Cowboy Roy says, "Noon stage runnin' late again?" I say, "Appears so, pardner," even though we have no stagecoach.

RULE #4 B.R.A.V.O.

What is B.R.A.V.O.? Dad says a successful theme park must have B.R.A.V.O.

B for Beauty

R for Rides

A for Adventure

V for Value.

When your hosts deliver all four your guests receive the lucky **O** for a Once-in-a-lifetime theme park experience.

These are Dad's rules. Whenever he recites them he finishes with a fist pump and a "BravO!" He tells me he's worked on these rules a long time. But I'm pretty sure he took them all from Disneyland.

The area behind the park, what we call backstage, is where the hosts take their breaks. That's where I am now, behind the North Pole in a pink mushroom-shaped hut trying to blink the toad dots from my eyes. I'm working on an idea in my Creative Arts notebook about snowflakes. Scientists say no two are alike. Thing is, how do they know if they haven't checked them all? I thought a comic about the FBI (Flake Bureau of Investigation) might have some potential. So I'm drawing variations of flakes when a head pops in the window. It's my best friend Britt Fairweather.

"Tree house?" he says.

"Tree house," I say.

We're making a tree house. Actually, we haven't started yet, but we've spent the last couple of days hauling supplies and tools out to an area behind the park called the North Woods. The woods go on for about a quarter mile or so and our tree house will be at the far end where hardly anyone ever goes, before where the woods become desert and rocks and nothing but desert and rocks for miles.

“Let’s see what you’ve got so far,” says Britt, nodding to my notebook. I show him my sketches.

He studies the seven sketches for about a minute then points at each one. “Junk, junk, junk, junk, junk, junk, and lemee see, hmm . . . Oh right: *junk*. Really, I am more than happy to help you with papier mâché,” he says.

I close my book and hide it in a crack in the mushroom wall. The thing with Britt, he cracks wise but in reality he’s pretty soft and gets bullied more than any guy I know, including me, so I cut him a boatload of slack.

“Let’s find my dad,” I say.

Dad is working with Hank the handyman on the refrigeration system at Charley’s Chocolate Factory. We’ve been having problems with melting candy. *Charlie and the Chocolate Factory*? True, that’s a book by Roald Dahl. But our Charley is spelled different. This is one of the unfortunate things about the park: the attraction names. When attendance fell and guests started calling Fairy Tale Place *Very Stale Place*, Dad updated a bunch of the attractions. Fear of what he called “frivolous litigation” kept him from using the real names, but it didn’t stop him from using variations of those names: the Sweet Dreams Candy Shoppe became

Charley's (with a Y) Chocolate Factory. The Little Bo Peep Hut became Shriek's Cottage (*Shriek*, the big *Blue* Ogre). The playground is called Lord of the Swings. The arcade is the Hunger Video Games. We have Star Trak, a rail ride, and Bart Sipson's Sippee Cup cart. Recently we were told by some lawyer to change the name of our Internet café, Charlotte's (Worldwide) Web. No one's told us to change the name of the diaper changing station, Winnie the Poo's, though I wish they would.

"Dad, can I cut out?" I say.

"Finish those toadstools?"

"Most of them."

"How about your Creative Arts assignment?"

"I'm working on it," I say, giving Britt a look.

"Be home for supper."

Hank offers us what looks like a melting brown potato. "Chocolate Oopah Loopah?"

Hank is covered from head to boot in chocolate and grease, the Oopah Loopah dripping down his arm.

"Hank, look at you," teases Dad. "You're a mess. You should get into a better line of work."

"What," says Hank, as he does a thousand times a day, "and get out of show business?"

Britt, me, and all the tree house supplies we can carry struggle on our bikes to the North Woods. As we pedal Britt is saying things like the tree house should be "architecturally balanced," "aesthetically pleasing," "green engineered," but I'm not really listening. I'm monitoring my front tire. Low again. It's got a slow leak Dad promised to patch, but until that time I pump it somewhere between two and two thousand times a day. I tell Britt I'll catch up as I hop off my bike to fish in my bag for the pump.

That's when I hear it. The horrible sound.

"Oh Brittany . . . *Yoooo hooooooooo.*"

Fifty yards up the road I see Hogg Wills swing down from a tree to body block Britt and his bike. Hogg, humongous, long fingernails, unwashed hair, stinky pulled-from-the-hamper-smelling clothes, nods at our supplies.

"Building a dollhouse?" he says, tipping Britt off his bike and onto the ground.

Tripp Vickles, Hogg's lackey, drops from another tree. "Did the girlie-girl dirty her girlie panties?" he says, watching Britt scrape at the mud on his jeans.

Bullies are dropping from the sky like frogs in a Bible story. I pray that's all of them, but mostly pray they don't hurt me too much as I come from behind my flat tire in what I admit is not so big of a hurry. But I'm saved when a car slows and Mr. Pennycross from the post office rolls down his window. "Hogg, Tripp. You boys playin' nice?"

"Oh, yes sir," says Hogg innocently.

"Good afternoon, sir," says Tripp.

"Howdy Britt," says Mr. Pennycross.

Britt stands and reclaims his bike from Hogg who was failing miserably at attempts to pop a wheelie. Britt walks it to Pennycross's car. "This is the new model, isn't it sir?"

"Why, no Britt. In fact it wasn't the new model when I bought her used four years ago."

"You'd never know it," I say, picking up my step. "You take good care of her."

Hogg and Tripp wait for Pennycross to leave, but Mr. Pennycross, wise to the ways of bullies, isn't budging.

"All right boys," says Mr. Pennycross. "Run on home now."

Hogg brushes past and whispers, "Better watch your back, Hobble." Part of me is hoping I don't lose my lunch and part of me is like, wow, Hogg Wills knows my name.

Tripp is taking his time. Mr. Pennycross asks if we'd like to hear the horn and he gives it a blast and Tripp stumbles on my two-by-fours. He quickly jumps up like he meant to do it and the two bullies storm down the street karate-chopping mailboxes and kicking trash cans.

Britt gives me the silent treatment the rest of the way. When we get to the tree house site I say, "When Tripp fell I should have said, 'have a nice *trip*.' Ho, ho."

Britt mumbles something while examining a rip in his snap-button shirt.

"What?" I say.

"I didn't say anything," he says.

I shimmy up the tree trunk, struggling with a two-by-four. Britt begins work on a walkway of stones. He gets the walkway sort of outlined, then takes a break to push a garden gnome up on the branch where I was planning to put the front door. A walkway? A garden gnome? I don't think Britt knows the first thing about tree houses.

"Hey, don't put that there," I say, but he gets the gnome stuck in a fork in the branch. I try to reach it, but my floorboards buckle, then my railing falls, then I do too.

The only thing left in the tree is that stupid garden gnome.

"If it's not in a tree can it still be called a tree house?" I ask. We had given up on the tree and built it on the ground.

"I think it's a fort now," says Britt.

I wanted to name it Fort Ninja. Britt "christened it" Fort Feng Shui after some term he'd read on the Internet. I'm calling it Fort Ninja.

Britt opens his backpack and takes out a miniature Mona Lisa painted by his father. I should mention his dad is a miniature artist. By this I don't mean to say he's a little man who paints; I mean he makes tiny pictures. Mini illustrations of the Last Supper or mini Minnie Mouse.

Britt hangs the mini Mona on the wall. It doesn't look so mini in our little fort.

Britt takes out a glass owl knick-knack and puts it on the windowsill.

"From my mom's collection," he informs me. But we're getting very un-fortlike with all this junk. "It's a little girlie," I say.

"I don't like that word," he snaps.

"What word?"

"'Girlie.' And major thanks for all your help today with Hogg and Vickles."

Okay, now it's coming out. I hoped he'd overlook that I seemed more interested in my flat tire than in joining him for a Hogg beating. I decide to address only the first comment. "Come on, when I say 'girlie' it's not the same as when that hog Hogg says it," I say.

No response from Britt. We're back to the silent treatment.

"Fine," I say. "I won't say 'girlie.' I have some girlie stuff too you know. *Dolls* . . ." Actually they're action figures, but I don't think I should put too fine a point on it at this moment.

"I think it stinks that you say that," he says.

"I *said* I won't say it. So sensitive. Jeez."

We sit through a few seconds of what they call an Awkward Silence.

"Are we finished?" I finally say. "Can we table it for now?" He doesn't answer. "Can we table it?"

"It's tabled! It's tabled!" he hollers. He's quiet for a minute, then pulls out some red curtains made from Elmo pajamas and kinda mumbles, "What do you think of these?"

"Nice," I say.

THREE

NEXT DAY I take my notebook from the crack in the Mushroom Hut and begin to rethink the snowflake story. By rethink I mean scrap it. Britt's right. Junk. I'm thinking maybe photography now. I like photography. At the park we have a Lost and Found: mostly sunglasses, ball caps, once a pair of dentures, and a few old Polaroid cameras from the 1990s. A Polaroid camera takes cool pictures that look like Instagram.

Problem is all of our film is old so sometimes the pictures don't turn out.

Sometimes they do.

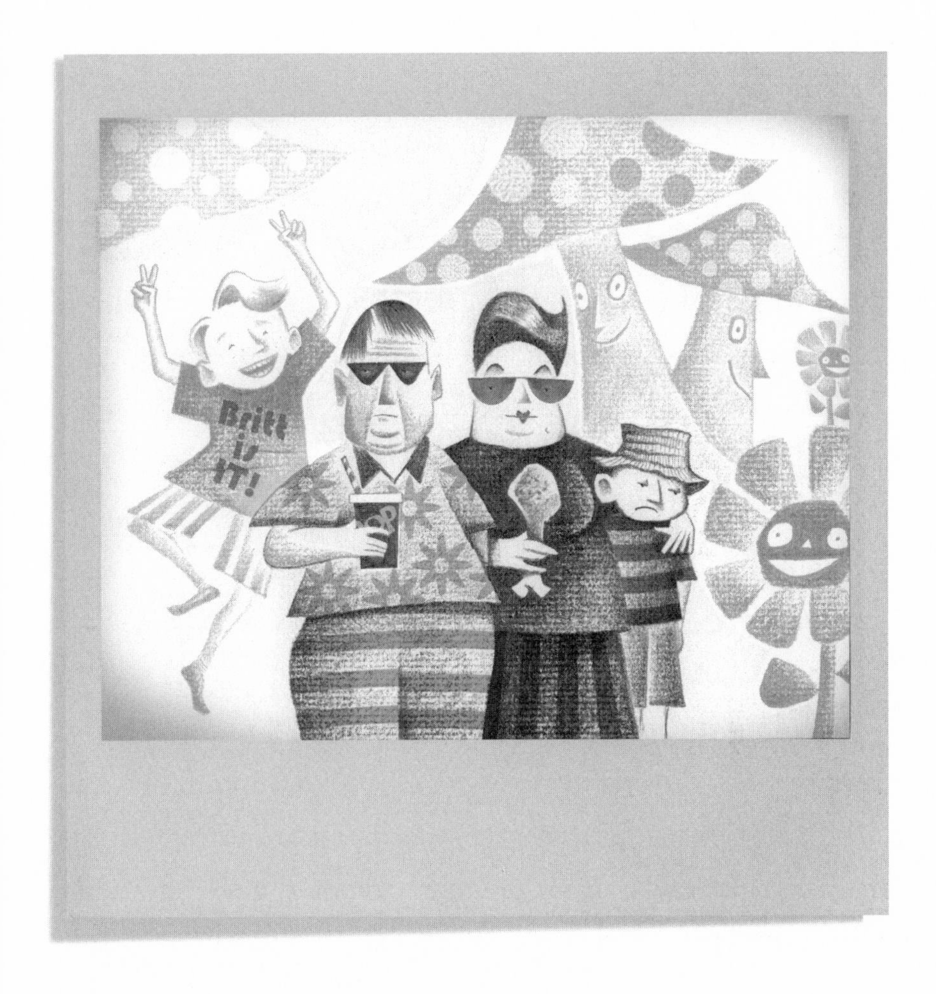

I have some time before my project is due, so if I get enough pictures together maybe I can turn them into a photo essay.

I take some shots of Cowboy Roy outside of Fort Fortitude. He's my favorite host. He does pretty cool rope tricks and he's a real good yodeler. He moseys—cowboys don't walk, they mosey—over to me. "Howdy pardner," he says. He wears denim jeans with buckskin chaps. He wears a bandana around his neck. He has boots with spurs and a shirt with fringe. I'm not good with ages, but he looks fairly oldish: twenty-four or twenty-five if I had to guess.

"How're things back at the ranch?" he asks. He means my house, but he calls everyone's house a ranch.

"Pretty good Cowboy Roy. How are things with you?"

"Fair to middlin'."

One of his duties is to lean on a split rail fence and recite cowboy poetry or recount western lore. "Swappin' lies and tellin' tales" he calls it. Most guests listen for a few minutes or shoot videos with their phones till they realize how long-winded he is, then move on. It doesn't seem to bother Roy. He could talk to twenty people or one.

Dad sees me and calls me over. "Augie, have you met our Summer Cinderella?"

He steps aside and I see it's Juliana, THE Juliana, a very popular girl from my school. What is *she* doing here?

"Cinderella," says Dad. "May I present my son, Augie."

"Nice to meet you, Augie," she says.

"Hi. We've met before actually," I say.

"Refresh my memory. Was it at my enchanted castle? Or in Happy Forest perchance?"

"Algebra. I sat behind you."

Perchance? She's obviously been through host orientation. I can't tell if she is staying in character because she really has no clue who I am or because she is embarrassed I know her from remedial algebra.

"BravO!" says Dad with a fist pump, walking away. When Juliana turns I sneak her picture.

"Hey princess," says a teenage guest wearing a Route 666 T-shirt. "Kiss any frogs lately?" Cinderella only smiles and dances away leaving the guest to turn his attention to me. "What are you looking at?" he says. I want to say I'm look-

ing at someone who obviously hasn't studied his princess stories, but when I see his skull-with-knife-through-eye tattoo I decide to dance away too.

Back in the Mushroom Hut, I take an extra long break and write a story in my Idea Notebook.

ONCE UPON A TIME CINDERELLA LIVED IN A FANCY CASTLE. YES, SHE LIVED IN A FANCY CASTLE WHERE SHE SCRUBBED THE FANCY FLOOR, COOKED THE FANCY MEALS AND CLEANED THE FANCY DISHES.

BUT ONE DAY SHE GOT A BREAK.
SHE GOT A VISIT FROM A FAIRY GODMOTHER.

THAT FAIRY GODMOTHER GAVE HER A FABULOUS MAKEOVER JUST IN TIME FOR THE ROYAL BALL. CINDERELLA JUST KNEW SHE WAS GOING TO DAZZLE THE VERY SINGLE PRINCE IN HER SHINY NEW DESIGNER GOWN AND SHOES. OF COURSE HE'D ASK HER TO MARRY HIM AND THEY'D LIVE HAPPILY EVER AFTER.

ALL WAS GOING WELL UNTIL CINDERELLA ARRIVED AT THE BALL IN HER BEAUTIFUL GOWN AND SHINY GLASS SLIPPERS.

THAT'S RIGHT, *GLASS!*

THE SECOND HER SHOE HIT THE PAVEMENT IT SHATTERED INTO A MILLION SHARDS CUTTING THE MAIN ARTERY IN HER FOOT, THE DORSALIS PEDIS. BLOOD SQUIRTED IN EVERY DIRECTION SPRAYING GUESTS WITH RED.

THE ROYAL CROWD YELLED ROYALLY RUDE THINGS . . .

CINDERELLA CRIED FOR HER FAIRY GODMOTHER BUT THAT GODMOTHER WAS SO EMBARRASSED SHE STAYED FAR, FAR AWAY. CINDY CLICKED HER HEELS TOGETHER AND SAID, "I WANT TO GO HOME!" BUT THIS ONLY SHATTERED HER OTHER SLIPPER CUTTING A BUNCH MORE ARTERIES.

THE HANDSOME PRINCE ARRIVED TO HELP BUT SOON HIS ELEGANT SUIT WAS AS BLOOD RED AS HIS ANGRY, RED FACE.

THE BAD NEWS: BY THE TIME SHE GOT OUT OF THE EMERGENCY WARD THE BALL WAS OVER, SO . . . CINDERELLA DID NOT MARRY A PRINCE, CINDERELLA DID NOT BECOME A PRINCESS AND CINDERELLA DID NOT LIVE HAPPILY EVER AFTER.

THE GOOD NEWS: CINDERELLA DID RETURN TO THE ROYAL CASTLE. IN ADDITION TO HER REGULAR CHORES AT HOME, CINDERELLA WAS MADE TO SCRUB THE BLOODY ROYAL CASTLE IN HER SPARE TIME.

FOOT NOTE:

SOON THEREAFTER, THE FGA (FAIRY GODMOTHER ASSOCIATION) RECALLED ALL GLASS SHOES. FROM THAT MOMENT ON FAIRY TALE SHOES COULD ONLY BE MADE WITH MATERIALS APPROVED BY COBBLER ELVES.

Mr. Tindall may like this because A) I discovered a flaw in the original story—glass shoes—and B) I elaborated on it. He is always telling us to elaborate on things. He might also like that I used "Dorsalis pedis," the only thing I remember from last year's biology class.

That evening when Britt and I come through the door Mom asks if I've come up with a project yet. I read her "A Cinderella Story." But instead of complimenting me on my dorsalis pedis, her only comment is that a real woman wouldn't waste her time wishing for a prince to solve her problems and I should keep working.

In my room I keep working.

Britt flips through a library book called *Mysterious Sightings*.

"You'd think they could take one shot in focus. Just one." He holds up the book. "Check it out, Bigfoot, out of focus. UFO, out of focus. Yeti, out of focus. Chupacabra, out of focus—"

"Chupacabra?"

"Bigfoot of Mexico."

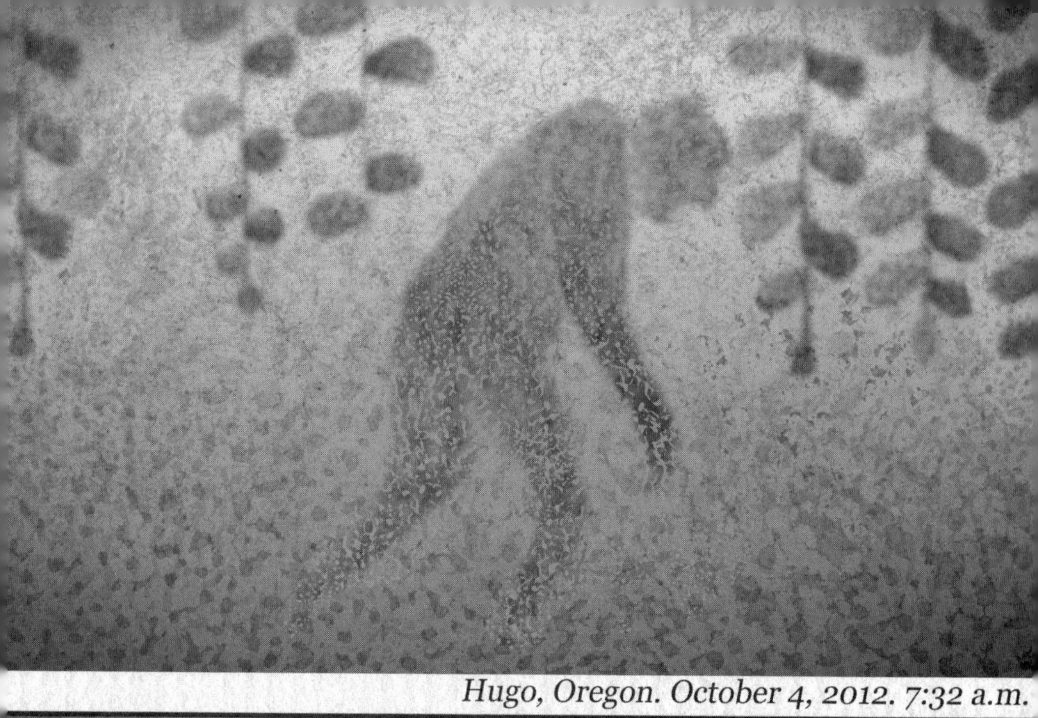

Hugo, Oregon. October 4, 2012. 7:32 a.m.

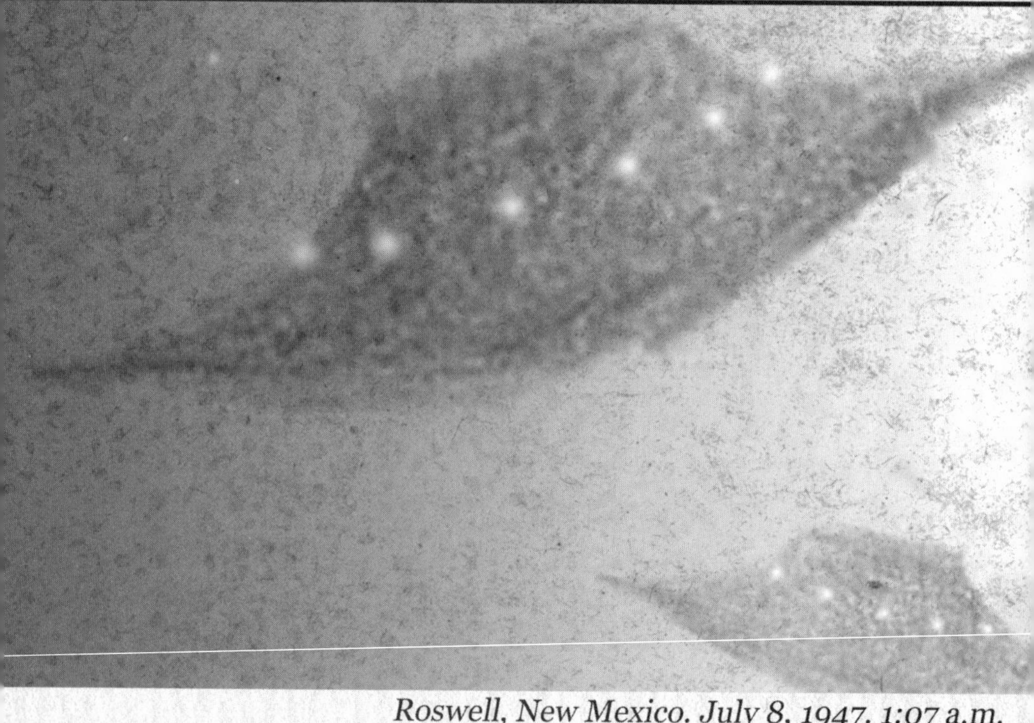

Roswell, New Mexico. July 8, 1947. 1:07 a.m.

London, England. March 2, 1992. 11:37 p.m.

Loch Ness, Scotland. December 6, 1933. 6:54 a.m.

I offer him half of my cracker. He starts to take it then stops. "Does that have rice in it?"

"Probably, it's a rice cracker." He goes back to reading. He's got allergies.

"Space alien," he continues, "out of focus. Loch Ness Monster, out of focus . . ."

"Nessie is probably my favorite monster," I say.

"I like the monsters in the old black-and-white movies like Frankenstein's monster with all those stitched-together body parts," Britt says.

This gives me an idea.

MISS EE-YUSS

by AUGIE HOBBLE

MISS EE-YUSS WAS ONE VERY MIXED-UP GIRL. SHE WAS MADE UP OF ALL DIFFERENT KINDS OF PARTS. HER FEET WERE ON HER HEAD. ON ONE FOOT SHE WORE A WOOL STOCKING, ON THE OTHER A WHITE ATHLETIC SOCK WITH A STRIPE. ON HER ELBOW BALANCED HER HAT WHICH WAS BLUE AND AROUND HER WAIST, A SCARF WHICH WAS RED AND DIDN'T MATCH THE HAT OR ANYTHING ELSE ON HER. SHE HAD ONE BROWN EYE, THE OTHER GREEN. SHE WORE JEANS AND OVER THEM, A DRESS THAT WENT ALL THE WAY DOWN TO WHERE HER HANDS TOUCHED THE GROUND.

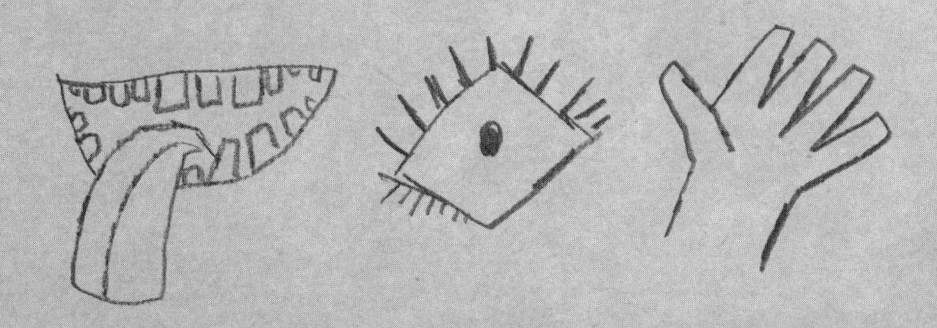

YES, MISS EE-YUSS WAS A VERY MIXED-UP GIRL. THAT'S PROBABLY HOW SHE GOT HER NAME: MISS ELAINE EE-YUSS.

I read it out loud to Britt.

"Miscellaneous? You're *absolutely* sure you don't want me to help you with papier mâché?" he says.

FOUR

AT THE END of every month Dad looks at the park attendance numbers and at the end of every month Dad freaks out. During these freak-outs he sits at his desk writing stuff on a notepad, erasing this stuff from the notepad, writing new stuff on the notepad, calling Hank on his cell, telling Mom he won't be home for supper, texting Hank on his cell, snapping at anyone who crosses his path, and generally driving everyone out of their birds. And by the end of the night he might come away with one or two of what he calls "guest enticements."

Example: Wet 'n' Wacky Week. This was Hank and me spraying guests with water misters. They were supposed to provide relief during the hottest week of August, but half

of the time we couldn't get the water pressure right so for the guests it was like going through a car wash with no car. They hated it. One Goth girl gave Hank a black eye.

Sometimes a guest enticement becomes a permanent attraction. Case in point: The Great Route 66 Dustbowl Adventure. This should've had a limited run but it's still here, not far from the real Route 66, which has been abandoned for years but was once the most famous highway in the world. The Mother Road. The road Okies and Arkies took to California for a better life during the great dust bowl of the 1930s.

Today the real 66 is mostly faded asphalt and weeds. Our 66 is not that different. Guests travel in tiny jalopies on a tiny highway while electric fans blow dust on them. This didn't work with water during Wet 'n' Wacky Week. I don't know why Dad thought dirt would be any more appealing. Not only do the guests get dust in their eyes and hair

and cameras, but the tiny cars always stall around tiny Tucumcari when their tiny motors get so clogged they have a tiny breakdown. Hank made anti-dust guards for the cars, but the attraction attracts few. Maybe it's too much of a bother to take it down and maybe Dad should've run it by Oala the Oracle before he ever put it up. Our fortune-teller might have told him the people who closed down the real 66 maybe knew what they were doing.

Oala, by the way, is a new "guest enticement" herself. She came to us from a bankrupt circus. Her troupe took a Greyhound home, but Oala and her daughter stayed. They met with Dad and hatched up the idea for Gypsy Camp right there on the spot. The daughter, Nicoletta, doesn't do much and doesn't talk much, but Oala makes up for the two of them with her endless predictions, hunches, and theories.

So now Britt and I are looking at a freshly painted sign advertising Dad's latest guest enticement: a Halloween-themed week-long event called Scary Tale Place. I have to say, this one might work. The park is pretty scary already.

Meanwhile from behind us comes the sound of glockenspiels. We may be talking Halloween, but here at the North

Pole it's Christmas every day. It's three o'clock so Wanda Jean and Sharon Jean in matching elf hats are starting "The Twelve Days of Christmas."

"Bet you a buck this song names at least six kinds of birds," I say.

"'Twelve Days of Christmas'? Bet you a buck it doesn't," says Britt.

Heh, heh. I listen to this song every day. It's lousy with birds.

On the first day of Christmas,
My true love sent to me,
A partridge in a pear tree.

"That's one," I whisper to Britt.

"Everyone knows the partridge," he says.

On the second day of Christmas,
My true love sent to me,
Two turtle doves,
And a partridge in a pear tree.

"Forgot about the doves," he says.

He must've also forgotten about the *three French hens* and *four calling birds* because when I ask him if he thinks "my true love" has some serious bird issues he doesn't answer, then after the *six geese a-laying* and *seven swans a-swimming* he takes the little hand towel from my custodial belt and tosses it to the ground. Throwing in the towel. I get it. Ha.

Victory.

"I'll take that dollar now," I say.

"We didn't shake on it," he says.

We never shake on it. I go to the custodial closet and get my pan and broom. Britt heads home. He's almost out of view as the elves sing the final verse, the one about the *twelve drummers drumming.*

He yells to me, "Maybe the drums'll scare away all the freakin' birds."

I take Lilliput Lane to avoid Birthday Town. "The Twelve Days of Christmas" once a day is one thing, but "Happy Birthday to You" five hundred times a day is depressing when it's not your birthday. I make a left at Shriek's Cottage, then take a shortcut through the fifteen-foot door called the DumbleDoor. I come out at Storybook Village. Jim, a sweeper with "seniority," tells me there's an accident near the twisty, turny Winding Nemo ride. What he means by "seniority" is that he's worked at the park longer than me and this somehow entitles him to skip "accidents." What he means by "accidents" is barf.

"I suppose I'm cleaning it up," I say.

"Weelllll . . ." he says handing me a packet of Pixie Dust.

Pixie Dust is what we use on throw up. It's pink and very absorbent. I sprinkle some on the bits of upchucked hot-dog, Oopah Loopah, and Ambrosia Punch, sweep it into my pan, then deposit the now semisolid pinkish patty through the mouth of a clown-head garbage can. A skinny, goofy-looking teenager wanders over. He wears a red hoodie even though it's ninety degrees. I gesture for him to lift his foot and I sweep up a paper napkin.

He says, "Can't go home till the paperwork is done, huh?"

"Ha, ha," I say, even though I've heard that one before. I pick up a popcorn box.

"How's business? Picking up?" he says.

Again, heard it. "Ha, ha," I force laugh. Us hosts are easy targets for guest humor, but I know the rules. I'm always polite.

Moze in the Big Bad Wolf suit walks out from behind Humpty Dumpty's wall.

"Hey Wolf," says Hoodie, "where's the three pigs? Afraid they'd *hog* all the attention?"

Moze puts his hands on his belly and mock laughs.

"Hey Wolf, I think I saw them at the Storybook Stage," says Hoodie. "They were doing *Ham*let."

Moze pantomimes searching for his pigs. He whips quickly toward the Storybook Stage and his oversize tail swats Hoodie to the ground. Moze clutches his cheeks, miming fake shock. I've seen him perform this tail maneuver before. It's a way of K-Oing a guest and making it look like an accident. Sometimes it's your only defense, like if you're being pummeled by a bunch of punks, but there's no reason to do that to a nerd with bad pig jokes. Moze skips away and I help the guy up.

"Someone should fix that tail. Major costume flaw," he says.

I sweep my way to Enchanted Castle hoping for another glimpse of Juliana. I'm behind Jack 'n' Jill's wishing well scanning the royal courtyard when I'm busted.

"Is thouest following me?" says Cinderella, coming out of the castle.

I get flustered. "No, I was just—"

"I'm but teasing, fair lad."

There are guests around so Juliana's in character. She points to my pan and broom.

"What manner of strange tools might these be? Such wonders."

I point to each. "Pan. Broom."

"Why, if only I had had such modern fare back in my days toiling for Stepmother. Bad times." She fans herself melodramatically. "But when life got me down, do you know what I did?"

"Huh uh . . ."

"I met my secret prince in the woods for a moonlit waltz," she says all sing-songy. "'Twas a welcome break from the drudgery of waiting on ugly stepsisters."

The guests chuckle.

"So what say you fair prince? A dance? Perchance tonight in Happy Forest?"

Being the center of attention always makes me uneasy. I smile and try to pass.

"I didn't catch your answer, noble prince."

"Hey, prince, answer the lady!" says a guest, egging me on.

"Sorry, uh, can't do Happy Forest. I got a thing in the North Woods tonight," I say, trying to play along.

"Oh, *this* princess is not picky. Any abundantly forested area will suffice."

The guests go, "Woooo," and snap pictures. I turn red.

"Let's see . . ." says Cinderella. "We should allow enough time before that pesky clock strikes twelve of course . . . my pumpkin coach has an expiration date . . ." She taps her chin, thinking. "Hmm . . . how's 8:32?"

"No problem," I say, trying to act casual in spite of my red head.

"Then it's a date," she says. "North Woods, 8:32."

She bows and floats away and the guests give me a round of applause. How embarrassing.

Thank goodness it's the end of my shift. I swing by the Mushroom Hut, grab my notebook, and head to the backstage vending machines. I'm a little flustered. I need a milk or something. I get a cold milk and sit taking deep breaths.

The break room door opens. It's Juliana. She plops down on a picnic bench and begins powdering her nose. I think maybe she doesn't notice me sitting behind her, but then in her non-Cinderella voice she says, "Hey, good work out there Prince Charming."

"Ha," I say. "Anytime."

"'Got a thing in the North Woods.' Pretty good," she says, snapping her compact shut. "What time did we agree on, 8:32?"

I spill my milk all over the place. I take the towel from my belt and sop up the mess. I kneel to get the rest off the floor. "I didn't think you were serious about our meeting—" I say but stop when I see her legs walking through the exit door back to the park.

More deep breaths. Did she just confirm a possible date or was she just rehashing our on-stage banter? Do I ask her? I'm not going to ask her.

Awkward.

Could be a major miscommunication. *Actually* . . . I pull out my notebook. I've been toying with the idea of a mural for my Creative Arts project. I look at the school building shots I took the other day. My mural was going to be about communication but maybe miscommunication is even better. On building one I could paint a guy on a cliff yelling something like, "How do I get to the other side?" On building two I'll paint a second cliff with another guy answering, "You're *on* the other side!"

SCAFFOLD HERE ?

15'

5 GALLO
ACR

LIBRARY

HELLOOOO! HOW DO I GET TO THE OTHER SIDE?

YOU'RE ON THE OTHER SIDE!

MURAL IDEA

This has potential. But I'll keep working on other ideas in case I can't get permission to paint on the library and the principal's office. I stuff my book in my bag and head for the park exit.

What time did we agree on, 8:32? The sentence keeps repeating in my head as I bike home. Was she serious about a date? Naw. Just staying in character. Kinda specific though. 8:32, she said. Maybe she's just not that great at improv. I turn off the road and pedal to a long, flat, turquoise building. It's where Mom works. Southwest Art and Gemstone Emporium. I park under a sign that says OBJECTS D'ART but truth is the shop mostly sells the kind of polished rocks people buy on vacation then toss in a drawer once they're home. Mom looks up from her desk when the little bell over the door rings.

"Well, look who's here," she says.

I give her a hug and stand in front of the AC cooling off. I want to ask her about Juliana but who talks to their mom about stuff like that? I hem and haw then show her my idea for the mural instead. Mom tells me it's a nice concept but doubts anyone would let me paint on school property.

The bell tinkles again and a big man in plaid shorts and sandals over black socks enters.

"Howdy," he says. "I'm in the market for a carved coyote."

Mom greets him and walks to a large canvas. "I have this painting of a coyote."

He eyes it taking a sip from his Stuckey's thirty-two-ouncer. "Naw, got my heart set on a carved one."

"Did you try Santa Fe? Or online?"

He moves to a painting in the corner. "Look at this 'un," says the man. "Whimsical. Yes sir, whimsy ta spare. Look at these little dudes holding up that rainbow."

"Those are Native American spirits."

"Tell you what, I'll think about it. Now can I show *you* a picture?" He reaches into his shirt pocket and pulls out a photo. "Seen this person around?"

"You police?" asks Mom.

“How ’bout you?” he says, showing me the photo of a boy eighteen or so. I shake my head.

“I’m sorry, I don’t mean to be a noodge here but can we see a badge or something?” says Mom.

He flashes a very official-looking badge but it’s back in his pocket quicker than you could blink.

“No need no one gettin’ hot under the collar, ma’am,” he says, smiling. He rubs the back of his neck. “But she sure is a hot one today, ain’t she?”

“What’s he done?” asks Mom. “The boy in the picture.”

The man takes a loud *sluuuuuuurp* from the last of his thirty-two-ouncer and buries his hand in a bin of polished stones. He brings it back up, the pebbles dropping through his fingers until only one is left in the center of his palm. “Oh, not much. But I wouldn’t mind conferring with the boy before he does much more. Call it a preemptive action if you like.” He studies the pebble before tossing it back into the bin. He tips an imaginary hat, says “Ma’am,” and walks to the exit in those socks and sandals. "Might come back for that rainbow painting," he says over the tinkling doorbell.

Mom turns to me. "See what I tell you kids about getting into trouble?" she says.

"I didn't do anything."

"I know, sweetie," she says, kissing my cheek. "And you better not."

Most people complain about the weather. My dad complains about the weatherman. At home that evening we're all watching the news when Dad starts his usual rant. He says the weatherman spends too much time on birthdays and stuff no one cares about and not enough time on the weather.

It gives me an idea for a cartoon.

WHAT THE WEATHERMAN SAYS:
IF YOU LOOK AT OUR DOPPLER MACH IV MULTISCREEN, YOU'LL NOTICE THE TEMPS ARE LOOKING SULTRY. SPEAKING OF SULTRY, HOW ABOUT MARY BETH GILROY? HOO-HAW! 21 TODAY! A BIG BIRTHDAY SHOUT-OUT TO HER. AND IN CLOVIS, CLOCKING IN AT 79 YEARS YOUNG, PAULINE KIRBY. PAULINE, YOU DON'T LOOK A DAY OVER 78! HEH HEH. NOW WE'VE GOT A PESKY STORM OVER TEXAS THAT MIGHT BRING SOME DOWNPOURS OUR WAY ON I-40 BUT YOU KNOW WHAT THEY SAY ABOUT OUR WEATHER: IF YOU DON'T LIKE IT, WAIT 10 MINUTES! HOO-HAW! MORE IMPORTANTLY, DON'T FORGET TO SEND IN THOSE PET PICS WITH FIDO OR FELIX DRESSED AS THEIR FAVORITE TV-3 PERSONALITIES. AFTER THE BREAK, I'LL BE SHOWING THE ENTRIES WE'VE RECEIVED SO FAR, AND IF WE HAVE TIME, YOUR 5 DAY FORECAST.
3
WHAT THE WEATHERMAN SHOULD SAY:
IT'S GOING TO RAIN. TAKE AN UMBRELLA.
3

As I draw, the weather guy yammers on about the phases of the moon. There's going to be a full one tonight. He never even gets to the forecast. Dad gets so mad, he stands up and throws his *Theme Park Monthly* at the screen, then when he sits back down all the park keys in his pockets fall between the cushions, making him madder.

At eight I ask Dad if I can run over to Britt's for an hour or so. He looks to Mom, but she's already conked out on the couch. He says okay, but just for an hour.

I pump up my bike tire and head for the North Woods.

The woods are covered in fog. The weatherman-who-never-gets-to-the-weather didn't say a thing about this. I lean against a tree squinting for Juliana and trying to look cool, but it's kinda hard to look cool when you're glancing at your watch every other second. Here's my thinking: if Juliana was serious about a waltz in the woods, then her Prince Somewhat-Charming is here. If she was just doing her Cinderella act at least I haven't embarrassed myself: "Uh, just to confirm, Juliana, you *were* serious about getting together later as oh-so-suited-for-each-other boyfriend/

girlfriend weren't you? If not I of course totally understand you were just doing that princess thing you do which is totally fine as well. I'm just, you know, a bit of a stickler for details and— "

And it's 8:58. Who am I kidding? She's not coming for any waltz.

Definitely not.

Better give the area one last scan though.

Nothing.

Nothing but blue. Blue because of the thicker-than-ever fog.

Blue trees.

Blue rocks.

Blue full moon.

Blue everything.

Everything but that flash of red.

Juliana?

No, a guy. It's that nerdy hoodie guy in his red hood. Running crazy like my Aunt Mavis's old banty rooster on chicken night. "Hey!" I yell. He can't hear me, that stupid hood covering his ears. "Hey!" I yell again. He's moving fast. Then behind him, another figure. A much bigger figure. Moze? In the wolf suit? This is a violation of so many of Dad's rules I don't know where to begin.

"Moze, you get that suit dirty my dad will kill you!" I holler. I follow them both.

I can barely see through the fog. I think I see Moze jump the guy.

I catch up, feeling my way through the fog. I follow voices until I hit fur. I find a furry arm and pull it hard, freeing Hoodie. "Go!" I say. He staggers to his feet and disappears into the fog. The arm twists around and pins me. I see big white teeth dripping with slobber. The disgusting slobber rains down on my face. I realize I'm near Fort Ninja, our on-the-ground tree house, and I knee him in the gut and run. I see the foggy triangular shape of the fort come into focus. I hear footsteps close behind. I dive through the front door and roll inside. I slam the door and scoot a folding chair against it. I hear clawing at the cheap plywood. I feel like the little pig who built his house of sticks. Should have used bricks. The door is pushed in by a hairy arm that drags me out. I feel myself being lifted into the air, then thrown against a tree with a force that makes the whole trunk shake. Is the fog getting foggier or is it me? Everything out of focus. The shadowy, fuzzy wolf shape lumbers toward me, arms outstretched. "Owoooooooooo . . ." he howls. Then something above is loosened from the vibrating tree. It falls and hits him square on the head.

He staggers back, shaking his head before limping off into the night.

I look down at the shattered pieces of plaster all around me. Saved by Britt's garden gnome.

I walk back to my bike. The tire is low and I have to push it all the way home.

I come through the garage door. Mom's still sleeping on the couch. Dad's still reading his magazine.

"I thought we said nine, sport," says Dad, barely looking up from his mag.

"Sorry. We lost track of time playing video games."

He glances over at me and sees my mussed hair and muddy clothes. "Some video game."

FIVE

NEXT MORNING. I feel like I'm covered in ants. It's 10 a.m. but already as hot as high noon. The AC in my room is broken. Dad says he'll fix it but all he ever does is click it on and off a few times and mumble "piece of junk" and say it's not that hot. So I'm all sweaty and itchy and when I feel my face it's like I have tiny splinters coming out of my skin which makes me more itchy. I grab Mom's leg razor from the tub. I rinse it off in hot water, then rake it over my chin a couple of times.

I get to the park with time before my shift starts, so I'm backstage in the break area reading a Wolverine comic book and drinking a Bart Sipson Sippee when Moze squeezes in next to me. I start to get up. He pushes me back down. He calls me an Indian. I ask why and he says cause my face is under "Heap big TP." I say that doesn't even make sense so he hits me in the arm and says, "Teeeee Peeeeee. Toilet paper, twerp." He goes, "Woo, woo, woo," and does a lame version of an Indian dance with an imaginary tomahawk. I say that's not very PC. He says, "PC, Mac, who cares?" and hits me again. Then he announces, "Survey time!" and asks what I think of "The Radz" for a band name.

Of *course* he's in a band. What a tool. "Rad? It's a little old school," I say.

"No, with a Z, turd. Radzzzzz."

"Hey, just so you know, I didn't tell my dad about you taking the wolf suit out of the park last night," I say, eyeing his head for garden gnome damage.

"I didn't take the suit out. How about Death Circuz?"

"The heck you didn't. That hoodie guy was scared witless."

"I was at band practice last night, dink-wad. Death Circuz or Radz?"

"Does everything have to end in a Z?" I say, annoyed. "How about Effluvium?"

"Effluvium?" he says.

"Yes, effluvium. It's like . . . like a killer virus."

"Killer virus. Yeah. The Effluviumzzzzzz."

He repeats it a few times, then punches me in the arm once more with enthusiasm. "I like it, Tonto."

Effluvium is the stuff they pump out of the park's septic tanks.

"I don't know if you could tell in all that fog but that was me you threw against the tree last night."

"You are *so* weird, Hobble. I have no idea what you are talking about."

He snatches the comic book from my hand and waves it over his head as he walks to the restroom. "Anyone needs me I'll be in the library," he says.

"Of *course* it was a werewolf," says Britt. "That kind of thing happens *all* the time in the woods of New Mexico."

"No reason to get all sarcastic about it," I say. "I'm just throwin' it out there. I told you I don't know what it was."

It's afternoon. We're repairing Fort Ninja.

"I thought you said it was that Neanderthal who is always picking on you. Moze."

"I thought maybe it was but I think he's too stupid to act dumb. He had no idea what I was talking about."

"Well, whatever it was, our fort was no match for it. And isn't that the one requirement for a fort? You know, to fortify?"

"I got some of its saliva on me." I touch my chin where my face splinters were. "I could be morphing into a Super Wolf or something. Like in an origin story."

"Uh-uh. Peter Parker gets bit by a radioactive spider and becomes Spiderman. You got slobbered on. If anything you'll turn into Slobberman."

"If I became a superhero I might even save your sorry butt from Hogg."

"*Sure* you would," says Britt in "that" voice again. "Augie, this is real life. In real life there are the Hoggs and there are the Augies. You'll always be an Augie."

"I wouldn't mind beating that guy once in my life. My *real* life."

"I have an even better idea. Let's not and try to make it through middle school alive."

“Hammer.”

He hands it to me. “Your hammer, Thor.”

“If I became a mutant or something scientists would have to put me on ice like E.T. Maybe freeze me like Walt Disney. Thaw me out in the future once they’ve figured out how best to use my super wolflike powers.”

“That’s a myth.”

“Government cover-ups? Ever hear of Roswell? Ever hear of Captain America?”

“No, that frozen Disney story,” says Britt.

“It’s not,” I say.

“It is,” says Britt. “The other day Principal Phillips announced a field trip to that show *Disney on Ice*. When he said *Disney on Ice*, you should’ve heard the snickers.”

“I don’t follow.”

“I’m saying everyone knows the urban legend of Walt Disney being frozen, so if you give a show a title like *Disney on Ice* you’re just asking for it.”

Britt takes back the hammer to pound a roof shingle but nearly takes his thumb off.

“Maybe there were snickers because ice shows are lame,” I say.

"Ice shows are not lame. Ice shows are cool," says Britt. "Stretchy tights are not cool."

"Robin Hood is not cool?"

"Robin Hood is cool. With all due respect, Robin Hood's stretchy tights are not cool."

Britt and I have seen a bunch of movies where they use this phrase, "with all due respect." You can say just about any awful thing to a person as long as you say "with all due respect" first.

"With all due respect, you're full of it," says Britt.

"With all due respect, you're full of it more," I say.

"With all due respect, I'm off to Yellowstone on Friday. Hee, hee."

It's true. Britt's family takes a two-week vacation every summer. Whenever I ask my dad why we never go on vacation, he says we are way luckier because every day in Fairy Tale Place is the best vacation a guy could wish for.

"Don't forget to bring me a present," I say to Britt with a big smile.

He smiles back. "You might get a little something."

Britt moved across the street from me in fourth grade. That week some big kids had taken his lunch money, so I gave him half of my tuna sandwich. He thanked me. I told him it was nothing. He said it wasn't nothing, it was something. I said, well, maybe a little something. Then I gave him my carrot sticks too. It didn't matter that I can't stand carrot sticks. It was the gesture. We get picked on, teased, made fun of, and beat up a lot. When you have that much in common with a person you kinda form a bond.

"If you could pick, what superpower would you choose?" I say.

"Invisibility," Britt says. "You?"

"Super strength I guess."

"Oh wait, I'd go with super strength too."

"Too late. You already said invisibility."

THIS IS AUGIE.
AVERAGE HEIGHT.
AVERAGE LOOKS.

AVERAGE.

BUT DON'T COUNT HIM OUT JUST YET, FOR BENEATH THIS AVERAGE APPEARANCE LURKS A NOT-SO-AVERAGE SECRET!

IT'S BEEN SAID A WOLF CAN HEAR A PIN DROP AT 3 MILES AWAY.

AHA!
I SEE YOU ATTEMPTING TO PICK THE LOCK WITH THAT SEWING NEEDLE! DROP IT!

BUT THE VILLAINOUS HOG-MAN THINKS FAST!

YES, AS EVERYONE KNOWS, WOLVES ARE CARNIVORES. THE MERE SIGHT OF A VEGETABLE WILL SEND SUPER WOLF INTO A TAILSPIN!

BUT WAIT...

IT'S BOY BRITT, AKA MR. MACHE!

THESE PAPER MACHE MONSTERS SHOULD SCARE THIS BULLY ALL THE WAY TO BULLIGARIA!

OH NO!
WE FORGOT MR. MACHE'S ONLY SUPERPOWER IS THE ABILITY TO CREATE PAPER MACHE!

THUS...

HOG-MAN MERELY TIPS BOY BRITT'S "MONSTERS" OVER WITH A DAINTY PINKY!

THEN...
GULP!

MR. MACHE, STIFF WITH FEAR, TIPS HIMSELF OVER!

BUT THIS DISTRACTION HAS BOUGHT OUR HERO TIME.

TIME TO CRAWL INTO THE LIGHT OF THE FULL MOON AND. . .

OOOOOWOO!

LOOKS LIKE HOG-MAN JUST WON A TICKET TO THE CARNIVORE CARNIVAL!
HOG-MAN, I'M GOING TO WOLF YOU DOWN!

AAARRRRR...

MY APPETITE WAS CARNI-VOR-ACIOUS!
BURP!

MY HERO! WHAT A SUCCESS!
YES, A HOWLING SUCCESS! OWOOOOO!
UGH, I'M GETTING AIRSICK . . .
THE END?

Britt leans back in our fort's wobbly chair, reading the Super Wolf comic I drew at lunch today. He actually gets a chuckle out of it even though he tells me I spelled papier mâché wrong.

We gather our tools, load up the bikes, then head home for supper.

SIX

AFTER SUPPER, DAD says he wants to drive to the park for a quick check of Charley's refrigeration system. I ask if I can tag along. I tell him I want to catch Cowboy Roy's latest rope trick, but really I'm thinking of Gypsy Camp and Oala the Oracle.

We get there and Dad tells me I've got one hour.

I jog to Gypsy Camp thinking Britt's right, we live in real life not make-believe—I turn left at Humpty Dumpty—but the thing is, if you have access to an oracle, what's the harm in running a quick question by her, however unrealistic?—I turn right at Shriek's Cottage—I mean, an oracle is way better than Google if you want answers.

I arrive at Oala's caravan and ring the bell. Her daughter Nicoletta answers.

"Hi. Talk to your mom for a sec?" I say.

Nicoletta just stands there fiddling with her troll doll necklace. The girl is weird. Hardly talks, never makes eye contact, and at eighteen, a little old to be wearing troll doll necklaces if you ask me. "Whatever," I say. I hear rustling in back, so I brush past, calling for Oala.

"One minute," Oala says from behind the curtains.

I hear the scratch of a needle on vinyl, then zither music.

"En*terrrrrr*," she says very mysterious-like.

I push back the curtain to find Oala surrounded by candles and seated at a crystal ball.

"You see Oala about face?" she asks.

"Face? What?" I touch the TP on my face. "No, I've been having some shaving . . ."

"Sit," she says. I sit. She waves her hands over the glass ball, squinting into it. "I see your bedroom. Is a mess. Clean it!"

She's giving me her usual spiel.

"Oala, I don't mean to be rude, but I'm not here for your act."

"Ball was fuzzy anyway." She gives it a few whacks and it blinks off.

"You *do* have seeing powers don't you?"

"I have seeing powers, never you mind."

She must see I look skeptical because she leans back in her chair and says, "Let me share example. The year, 1977. Young man comes to me. He has scratched LP record. *Bay City Rollers*. Why you come here? I ask. Young man wants to know should he upgrade to new invention: eight-track cartridge. But I divine change in future. I tell him, do not upgrade. I foresee eight-track having short life. Quickly becoming obsolete. I foresee something after called cassette tape. He asks, so I wait for cassette? I say, No, I see more. I see cassette too becoming obsolete. He asks, I wait then for . . . what? I say I see compact disc. He says, compact disc, aha, I wait for this? But again, I tell him, wait. Do not upgrade for I see more. I foresee CD too becoming obsolete. This man is going crazy. He has never seen such powers. So I tell him one last thing. I tell him of downloadable digital file for iPod."

"C'mon, this is 1977?"

"And that man's name? Steve Jobs."

"C'mon."

"Is true. I do not even tell him one day he will listen to *Bay City Rollers* on cell phone. I do not want to blow his mind."

"C'mon."

"You know what advice I give? I say hold on to record. Vinyl never go out of style."

"With all due respect, I should believe that?"

"Did it not all come to pass?"

Oh brother.

Oala pours a cup of tea. But she doesn't drink it. She throws it in the sink. She peers into the bottom of her cup. She pushes it away. "The tea leaves tell nothing. Let Oala see palm."

I give her my hand. She traces her finger along the lines.

"Oala, I only came here for a quick question. The other night, the night of the full moon, I came into contact with something and—"

Her left eye blinks. Only the left one. It's what they call a nervous tic. My uncle Jubal has it. I've seen him get it around snakes and fancy restaurants.

Oala looks at the clock. "Oala finished."

"Wait, I didn't get to my question. Oala, do you ever read comic books?"

"*This* is your question?"

"My question is if a guy came into contact with a wolf or whatever, is it possible that guy might, like in the comics, acquire some powers of that wolf or whatever? I know it's a long shot, but, you know, if there was a full moon and if the wolf slobbered on him maybe . . ."

"You waste Oala's time now. Tea leaf told nothing, crystal ball was fuzzy. Hand? Is fuzzy too."

I hold up my hand. "Wait a sec," I say. Then I see my hand *is* fuzzy. A couple of fuzzy hairs on the back of my hand I hadn't noticed before. I look at my other hand. Same thing. Oala pushes me out the door.

She's really anxious to get rid of me. Did Oala see the Super Wolf in me? From Fort Fortitude I hear Hank Williams on the scratchy loudspeaker singing about chasin' rabbits and howlin' at the moon.

I begin to trot. Hardly any guests in the park tonight, so I run. "Owooo!" I yell. I run through all four lands, not stopping until I reach the Bart Sipson Sippee Cup cart.

"Give me a 7-Up," I say, panting.

Libby, the vendor, fishes for one in the ice.

"You okay?"

"Don't . . . know," I say. "Better . . . give me . . . something . . . stronger. Make it . . . a Dew."

"She's a fake you know," says Libby, handing me the Mountain Dew.

"Who's a fake?"

"Oala," she says.

I hand her a dollar.

"I see things," she says.

"How did you know I was at Oala's?"

"I said I see things."

She's a little annoying, this one.

"To be clear, the soothsayer is a fake, but the fast food host knows all?"

"I'm not a fast food host, I sell beverages. And I didn't say I know all, I said I see things."

Annoying *and* specific. "Should I call you Claire?" I say maybe a little too sarcastically.

"For clairvoyant? Sure. You're going to anyway."

"You could see that, huh?"

"No, you just seem like the kind of jerk who would do something like that. I've worked here all year and you've said like three words to me in all that time."

"Sorry," I say. "Then let me say more words now: Does this hand look hairy to you? Because it sure spooked Oala."

"Oala didn't shoo you off because of that hand. She shooed you off because it was eight."

"What's that, a Gypsy thing?"

"Her *Toddlers & Tiaras* show comes on at eight."

"Naw. You think?"

"Yes, I *think*," she says, looking a little irritated. "I'll tell you what else *Claire*-voyant thinks. I think you like cats.

I think you like the Albuquerque Isotopes. I think you like comic books. I think you like pizza."

"You just described every kid I know. We were talking about my hand."

"I think you painted polka dots on the *front* of the toadstools only, not the back. I think you have a fort in the North Woods. I think you failed Creative Arts. I think you get bullied a lot. I think you like that airhead who plays Cinderella. I think you can't stand Moze. I think you are weird."

"Weird? As in superhero weird?"

"Weird as in Comic Con superhero weird. And that hand? You're no wolfman."

How did she guess this was what I was getting at? I back up and bump into that teenager from a few days ago. The one with the Route 666 T-shirt and skull tattoo. He's got a friend with him. The friend has some chin whiskers that look like the stuff we weed out of the Magic Tee House putting green.

They're blocking me. But I'm in no mood. I can sense Claire still watching too.

I look up to the moon.

I take in a long breath, then let it out.

"You don't want to make me mad," I tell them in my best Super Wolf voice. "You wouldn't like me when I'm mad."

They look at each other. Then burst out laughing.

"Oh man," says Whiskers. "Did you just quote a line from the Hulk?"

They give me a wedgie.

Claire calls to me from her cart, "I knew that would happen."

Some clairvoyant. She didn't even mention my tomorrow. Tomorrow, the day my entire future depends upon. The day I have to give Mr. Tindall my final project ideas.

SEVEN

UNDER NORMAL CIRCUMSTANCES Mr. Tindall's classroom is intimidating. He's got framed museum posters on the walls. Not thumbtacked, framed. *Monet at the Met*, *Gorky at MoMA*. He sometimes plays strange music as we take our seats: Stravinsky, John Cage, Björk. But today it's especially intimidating due to the absence of heads to hide behind. There are only a few kids here, which means we'll *all* get called on today. I head for my usual seat, but Tripp Vickles is sitting in it. I move to the far side of the room where Darla Gumm fiddles with the zipper on her accordion case. I glance a few seats over to Dewey Webster who is collecting wax from his ear. How did I get lumped in with these rejects?

Mr. Tindall looks very serious studying something on his laptop. He waits for us to take our seats, then stands and pulls down the projector screen. Spammit! This is going to be one of his PowerPoint demonstrations. He connects his laptop to the projector. "People, you are here because your final projects were deemed unacceptable," he says. "The good news? You all get a do-over." His laptop screen is projected on the big screen behind him. It says, RECONNECTING TO LAST PAGE VIEWED. The page loads. It's photos of kittens in little costumes.

"It doesn't have to be a painting or a drawing. It can be a song..."

Molly Dinkle laughs out loud as a kitten dressed as Beyoncé loads on-screen.

Mr. Tindall turns to the screen, then fumbles for his laptop escape key. "Stupid Wi-Fi," he says. We laugh and he adds, "Yes, it can even be photography. And these kitten photos of mine? The style is 'camp' and they are intended to be funny, so go on people, get it out of your systems."

We all crack up.

"All right, all right," he says quieting us down. "Maybe

we'll skip the PowerPoint and you guys simply tell me what you're thinking." He turns off the projector and scans the room. "Iris?"

"I plan on bringing in my Lego Star Wars collection."

"Iris, that's not a project."

"It's taken me three years. It's complete. I think it *is* a project."

"I printed out all the lyrics to Def Leppard songs," offers Tripp.

I laugh and he shoots me a look and I quickly turn my laugh into a cough like that's what I was doing all along.

"People," says Mr. Tindall. "You're missing an opportunity here. What we're looking for is something personal. Something that expresses who you are. Augie?"

"Well, to be honest," I say, "I'm having a hard time picking just one project. I have so many ideas."

"Enlighten us with one."

"Sure, uh..." I fumble with my project book. I can't decide. I panic! I'm a wiseacre around Britt, but when I get in front of people I freeze. My cheeks go red. My mind goes blank. "I was thinking about doing a . . . a . . . coyote carving." *A coyote carving? What am I thinking?*

"Like they sell in Santa Fe?" Mr. Tindall asks, confused.

"No, I mean a coyote story. Or a wolf story. Or a *song. Or story!*"

"Hobble, you need to focus and take this project seriously." He sighs and writes in his ledger, "Hobble. To be determined."

I get to my bike and squeeze the tire. It's fine.

"You gotta kick the tire." It's Tripp. He was waiting for me. He doesn't kick my tire. He kicks my foot. Hard. It smarts—must've hit the dorsalis pedis—then pushes me into a puddle.

"Ow," I say into the mud.

"Answer to the master," he says.

I have no idea what that means, but I'll bet it's a line from a Def Leppard song.

BASIC WOLF FACT
Wolves help keep ecosystems healthy an
in check. Wolves eat large
like deer, moose, and elk.
prey such as rabbits, beave
The reintroduction of the
a major success and toda
seen in their native habit
Wolves travel in p
Canis lupus: The scientific
Carnivore: An animal t
WOLF
Africa. They tend to live in the remote w
wolves prefer to live in swamps, coasta
Many people think wolves only live in
can live in temperatures that range fro
exceptional eyesight
oversize ears for acute hearing
strong thick neck
two hundred million smelling cells
long sharp teeth
large forepaws
body streamlined for speed

originally listed as subspecies or
cies in the contig
, we reclassifed t
ation at the speci
ontiguous United
esota gray wolf po
ed. Gray wolf popu
ns and Western Gr
2011 and 2012.

Werewolves Begat Werewolves

Folklore tells u
begat werewolv
physical encoun

1 The New South Wales Wolf

Wolves and the Food Chain

The rabbit eats the flower and the rabbit in turn is eaten
the owl. The owl is eaten by the wolf. This is the basic
of natur ... ator or prey. Eat or be eaten. The anima
kingdo ... of food chains. There are car

Alpha Male, Alpha Female, Beta, Omega

The omega is the most subordinate member of the pack. The weaker and smaller of the pack.
an the rest. Wolves occupying this lowly position rank lowest, typically due to size and strength. The

big bushy
tail
powerful
skeletal system
scent-making
gland to leave
scent trails
double layer
of fur
to protect
from elements
A Wolf on the Move!
A Mexican Gray Wolf has
traveled over 920 miles to the
astonishment of those studying
RED WOLF
The Wolf in Fiction
Gossop Wolfe thought to eat the little red
Riding-Hood but decided against it when
off in the distance he spied two hunters in
the forest. The poor child knew not what a
foul and dangerous
A program that saved the red wolf
from extinction could come to an
end. This week

That afternoon I hold an ice pack against my sore foot as I poke around the Internet reading about wolves. I print out a couple of pages. Then a couple more and before I know it my wall is full of printouts: behavior traits of the gray wolf, wolves and the food chain, wolf strengths, wolf powers. My wall is so covered I have to make a hole in an arctic wolf just to get to my underwear drawer.

I surf some comic book sites. I read about super strengths, retractable claws, x-ray vision, and flight. I read of freak lab accidents, gamma rays, radioactive spider bites, transformations. I type "wolf saliva." This links me to "wolf encounters," which links me to "werewolves."

> **Werewolf.** From Old English *were* for man and *wolf.* Also known as Lycanthrope. Mythological human with the power to transform into a wolflike creature. A werewolf is most often created through an encounter with another werewolf.

Comments:

2005MTM says:
If a werewolf comes after you stab it multiple times.

Saradactyl says:
u have to kill a werewolf with a silver bullet.

Freckles97 says:
Or chop its head off.

IttyBittyKitty says:
Beat it like a pinata. LOL.

Metalheadz13 says:
THIS SITE SUCKZZZZZZZZZZZZZZ.

LadiesLoveTodd says:
Technically, a vampire site would suck. A lycanthrope site would not.

IamOriginal says:
Death to all werewolves! Death! Death! Death! Death!

IamOriginal2 says:
If u r a werewolf, u WILL die. ☺

I then read an article that describes werewolves as "tortured souls cursed for all eternity." I don't like it. I can't be sure but I'm guessing a "tortured soul cursed for all eternity" is a lot less fun than a carefree Super Wolf.

Downstairs I hear my parents.

"Eight-letter word for husband," says Mom. She's doing one of her crosswords.

Dad spells out the letters. "H-A-N-D-S-O-M-E."

"Ha, ha. Clever," says Mom. "But I think it's 'partner.' No wait, that doesn't fit. One down, five letters: eccentric . . ." She pencils something in, then erases it. "Does Augie seem out of sorts to you?"

"Weird."

"Weird's a little harsh, Marty."

"No, five letters, W-E-I-R-D."

"Oh. That fits."

I move closer to the stairs.

"The wolf wall?" says Dad. "I saw it. All kids go through phases. When I was his age I had a Charlie's Angels wall. Same thing."

"Uh-huh," says Mom in her not-amused voice, "exactly the same. Capital of South Dakota."

"Pierre," he says.

"No, six letters."

"It's pronounced peer but you spell it like *pee-air*. P-I-E-R-R-E."

Dad puts down his *Theme Park Monthly*. He knows she's going to keep interrupting. He slides in next to her on the couch. "I wouldn't worry about Augie." He peeks at her puzzle. "Three across: Cooney who made Rumphius. I know this," he says. "B-A-R-B-A-R-A."

"What are you doing?" scolds Mom. "You know I like to do it myself."

I tiptoe back to my room and flop down in my beanbag. Gotta quit wasting time with this wolf stuff and get back to Creative Arts ideas. I take out my notebook. Cowboy Roy once said a good cowboy song should have horses, dogs, some gunplay, and love gone bad. Yodeling is good too if you can squeeze it in.

2 ACROSS, 1 DOWN (CROSS WORDS)

(A COWBOY SONG)

Lyrics by AUGIE HOBBLE

SAL RODE INTO TOWN,
ON HER H-O-R-S-E,
HER D-O-G BESIDE HER,
'TWAS AUGUST TWENTY-THREE.

TEX BROKE HER H-E-A-R-T,
ON THAT SUMMER DAY,
FOR HE WAS WITH ANOTHER GAL,
HER NAME WAS I-D-A.

CHORUS
CROSS WORDS, CROSS WORDS.
ANGRY WERE THEIR CROSS WORDS.
ANGRY, ANGRY CROSS WORDS.

SAL WAS PUZZLED,
HAD NO CLUE,
ON THAT D-A-Y.
SO SHE DREW A G-U-N,
THEN LEFT TEX THERE TO DIE.

YES SAL DREW HER G-U-N,
AND NOW THERE IS 1 DOWN,
WHERE 2 ACROSS THE ROOM ONCE
MADE EYES IN THAT TOWN.

SAL ASKED THE J-U-D-G-E,
WAS HER NUMBER UP?
HE SAID, WHY NO, DEAR CHILD,
I'M FRIENDLY AS YOUR PUP.

FRIENDLY AS YOUR PUP AM I,
GRACIOUS AND GOOD HEAVENS!
YOUR NUMBER'S NOT TO D-I-E,
YOUR NUMBER'S 5 2 7.

FIVE TO SEVEN YEARS FOR SAL.
CROSSWORDS AND A CELL.
DOIN' PUZZLES, DOIN' TIME,
NO PHONE CALLS, TEXTS OR MAIL.

CROSS WORDS, CROSS WORDS.
IF ONLY SAL HAD FLEW.
YEP, SHOULDA RUN,
NOT PULLED THAT GUN,
ON THAT LOUSY OH-DE-LAY-DE-WHOO.

(THIS LAST PART IS A YODEL)

The problem is I can't write music. And there's no way I'm getting together with Darla Gumm and that accordion of hers. It sounds like a chorus of asthmatic cats when she works that squeeze-box. Maybe best to leave it at what Aunt Mavis calls a "poim."

EIGHT

NEXT DAY I approach Libby the beverage host.

"I wanted to apologize for the other day," I say.

"I thought you might," she says.

"Here we go again."

"No, I mean you're not such a bad guy."

"Thanks."

"Although there is going to be another full moon in a couple weeks," she says grinning, "sooo, dot, dot, dot."

"You're making fun of me, aren't you, Libby?"

"I'm just messin' with ya. And you can call me Claire, it's kinda clever," she says. "You know, a full moon doesn't make werewolves. That's movie stuff."

"I know that." I didn't.

"Moonflower does."

"Moonflower?"

"Sure. Unlike your basic garden-variety flower, Moonflower blooms at night, most spectacularly under a full moon. Naturally, bigger moon, bigger light, bigger bloom. But most people still think: Full moon. Werewolf. The two have become synonymous."

"Sin on in . . ."

"It means 'associated with one another.'"

"I know what it means." I didn't. But I have a few fancy words myself. "So for all intensive purposes, if I go near Moonflower I might still become—"

"Intents and purposes," she corrects. "But like I said, you're no werewolf."

She was annoying me again. "Everyone is always correcting me," I say. "Here's a news flash, I'm no good with grammar. I'm a bad speller too. But you probably knew that already. Foresaw it or whatever."

She was smiling. "Hey, maybe sometime we could hang out or something."

"Hang out?"

"You know, maybe get an ice cream. Take a walk through Fairy Tale Place or dot, dot, dot."

We're interrupted by a kid getting more popcorn on the ground than in his mouth. I point to the mess, wave bye to Claire, and follow the kid. Just in time. Not sure how I feel about that last suggestion of hers.

I ask Dad if I can work in the Mushroom Hut after my shift. I have an idea for a story and since he still hasn't fixed the AC in my bedroom I hoped I could work on it without sweating all over my notebook. Dad says fine so long as I don't bug the other hosts.

I slip into the cool, dark hut. I look out its round window to the moon. I sit back and tear the lid off a twelve-pack of Goo Goo Clusters. Charley's was going to toss them, but the only slightly expired clusters taste just fine. I wash them down with a Dew. I take out my notebook and pens.

THE BAD SPELL

by AUGIE HOBBLE

EVERYONE AT MY PARTY GOT CAKE.
EVERYONE BUT ME.
IT WAS MY BIRTHDAY. WHERE WAS MY BIRTHDAY CAKE?
I JUST KNOW SOMEONE TOOK TWO PIECES.

THE BIRTHDAY MAGICIAN ASKED ME TO WRITE MY BIRTHDAY WISH ON HIS MAGIC TABLET.

I WROTE:

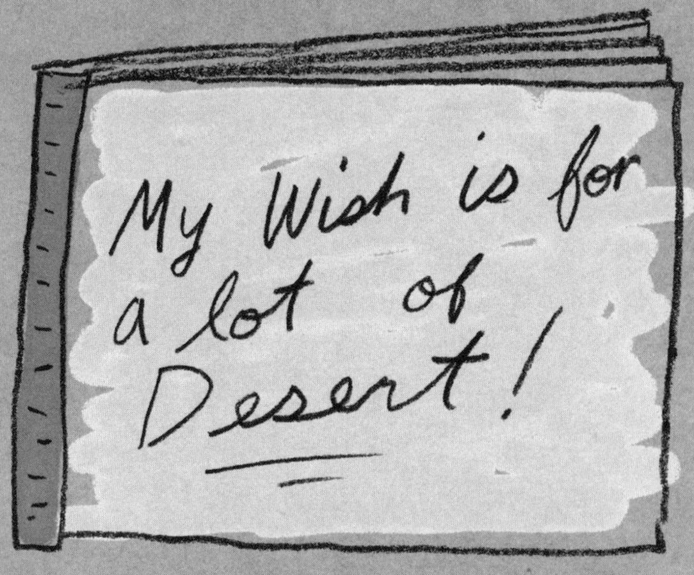
My Wish is for
a lot of
Desert!

HE TOLD ME TO CLOSE MY EYES AND COUNT TO THREE AND I WOULD HAVE MY WISH. "ONE. TWO. THREE," I SAID.

I OPENED MY EYES.
I WAS IN A BARREN **DESERT**.
MY WHOLE LIFE I HAVE BEEN A BAD SPELLER.
I HAD FORGOTTEN DESSERT HAS TWO S's.

IT WAS REALLY HOT.
DID NOT NEED HOT.
NEEDED COOL.
NEED COLD . . .

I CLOSED MY EYES. "ONE. TWO. THREE."
I OPENED THEM.
I WAS STILL IN THE DESERT BUT INSTEAD OF BEING CHILLIER I WAS HOTTER THAN EVER. I WAS HOLDING A BOWL OF STEAMING HOT CHILI!
I GUESS I SHOULD HAVE USED A Y INSTEAD OF AN I.

A BUZZARD FLEW OVERHEAD, THEN ANOTHER, THEN HUNDREDS! THEY SWOOPED DOWN AND PECKED AT THOSE CHILI BEANS AND WHEN THEY WERE DONE THEY PECKED AT MY BEAN.

I NEEDED A STRONGER HAT THAN THIS PAPER ONE. A BALL CAP. NO, A TOP HAT. NO, A BIG, THICK HAT. I SCRIBBLED MY WISH WITH A "ONE, TWO, THREE!"

"HO, HO, HO."
I HAD A CHRISTMAS **FIR** ON MY HEAD.
THE FUR I NEEDED IS SPELLED WITH A U
NOT AN I. I TOOK IT OFF AND SAID

This is harder than I thought. There are only so many words I can think of which are spelled two ways. A little hard to concentrate with my throbbing foot too. Tripp, that caveman. I pull out a picture I took earlier.

Weird girl. Kind of a pain in the dot, dot, dot.

My eyes close.

I open another Goo Goo. Then another. Then one more.

NINE

I MUST'VE FALLEN asleep in the hut. I awake to a closed park. I hop the locked main gate and stumble home to bed.

Next morning I come downstairs to find Aunt Mavis having biscuits 'n' gravy with Mom. Her eyes open wide like the painted ones on Li'l Bo Peep. What, is my barn door open? I check my pajama fly. But I'm not wearing pajamas. I'm still wearing my wrinkly clothes from yesterday. They're covered in dark stains. Goo Goo chocolate no doubt.

"Did you sleep like that?" says Mom, a little annoyed.

"I guess I did," I say, my cheeks turning color.

Aunt Mavis stands, shaking her head. "Well, bless his heart," she says, giving me a hug like I'm a moron or something. "I'll catch you later Mildred," she says to Mom, picking up her handbag and keys.

After Mavis leaves, Mom pours me a glass of juice and spoons some gravy onto a biscuit while she waits for an explanation.

"Sorry. I think I got home pretty late. Don't remember what time."

"Don't remember? My hunch is Mr. Pibb met Miss Goo Goo Cluster and had themselves a little party at your expense. I'm not going to tell you again to lay off the sugar. It makes you loopy."

I don't sass back, I just nod.

But if I *had* wanted to sass I certainly could've come up with something better than Mr. Pibb and Miss Goo Goo had a party: *Peppermint Patty* was looking for a *Sugar Daddy*. She didn't want a *Milk Dud*. On *5th Avenue* she saw *Mr. Goodbar* and blew him a *Hershey Kiss*. It caused him to *Snickers*. He thought her kiss was *Good & Plenty* so they were married and nine months later *Peppermint Patty* had twins: *Junior Mints*. The babies brought them *Almond Joy*. Except when the twins made *Skittles* in their diapers and—

"Augie, you're not listening to me are you?" says Mom.

"Yes I am."

"I said if you lay off the chocolate your skin would look better too. Maybe you wouldn't have all those tissues on your face all the time."

I act all interested in a story on Dad's iPad so she'll leave me be. The homepage of our local paper says the last few days have set a record for missing pets. A scientist from the college thinks it's because of climate change. The warm weather has messed with their inner clocks or something. They stay outdoors longer and sometimes don't come back at all. When Mom leaves, I pour myself a bowl of cereal. I quit the article and read the side of the cereal box. Ingredients: Oats, Dextrose, Marshmallow . . . Always thought marshmallow was spelled with an "e." Could use that in my spelling story: a marshmallow and a marsh that is mellow. Hmm . . . what other words? Led and lead. Stairs, stares. Principal, principle . . .

I shower, change, and head for the park. I have to walk because I couldn't get my bike past the locked gate last night. Along the way I count at least six "lost pet" posters. That scientist with the climate change theory might be onto something. I head for the Mushroom Hut. I take my notebook from my secret crack in the wall and open it to where I left off with the 'The Bad Spell' story. This is what I see:

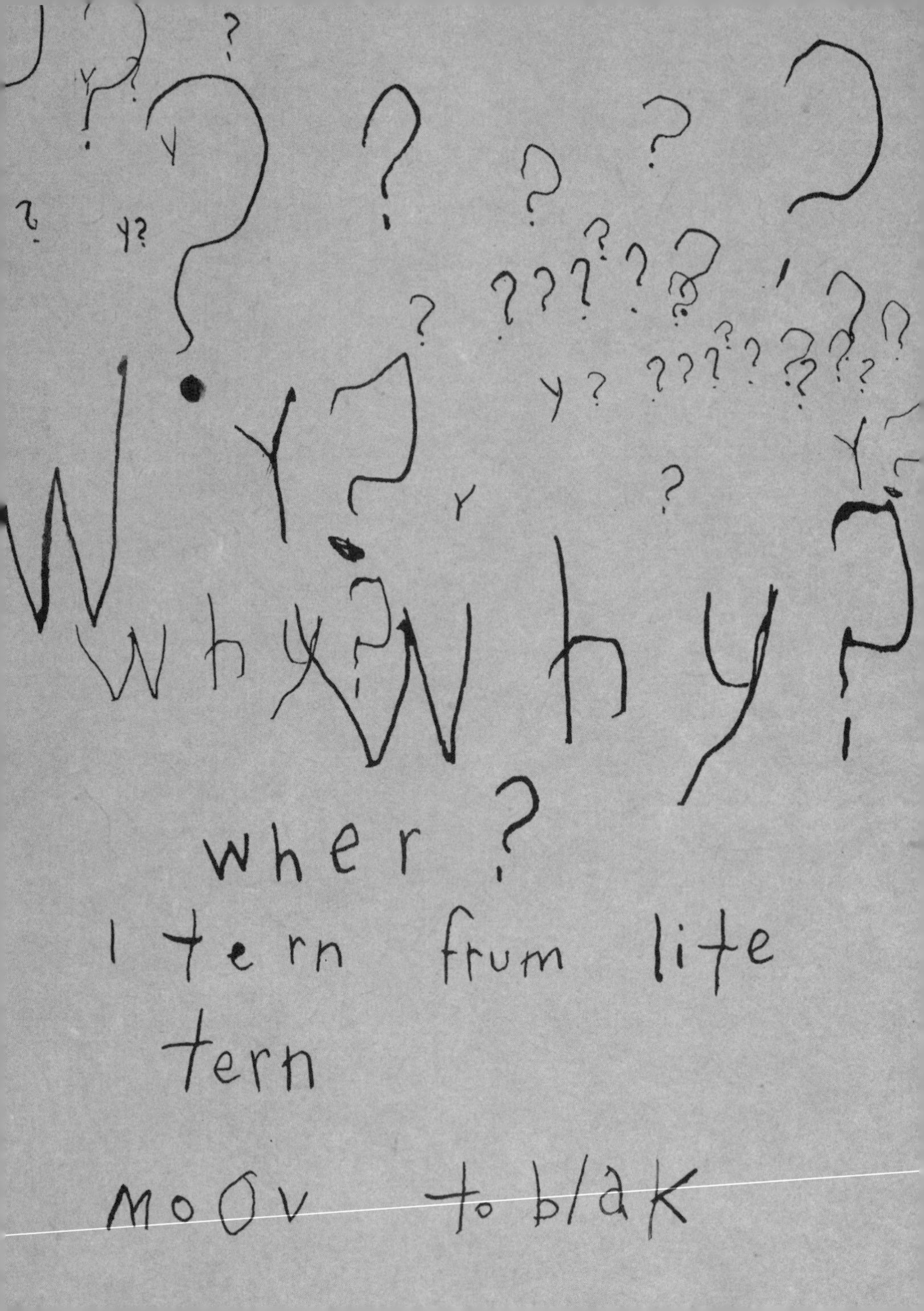
Why?
Why Why?
wher?
I tern frum lite
tern
mOOv to blak

muss getbak hom

instink

uUse instinc

mooy Lef movrite

thisway that

time meanless

wot happen mee?

???????

??

notno wherr am

?run irun feeleen verriweerd

weerd

weerd not shur y Dizzeeee zzzzz zzzzzzee

Okay. Maybe Mom has a point about sugar.

Thing is, this doesn't even look like my handwriting.

I track Moze down backstage. I confront him about the scribbles in my notebook.

"Looks like these were written by a dipwit," he says, examining them.

"So you admit it," I say.

He takes the cigarette out of his mouth to pop a stick of gum in. He puts the cigarette back.

"This book was hidden," I say.

"Hidden where?"

"Like I have to tell you about the crack in the Mushroom Hut."

"The crack in the Mushroom Hut."

"So you know about the crack in the Mushroom Hut."

"That book's gonna be up the crack in *your* mushroom hut if you don't get your face out of my face in exactly two seconds," he says, blowing stinky smoke all over me.

I start to leave. He yells, "I will say this: you better hide it in a better spot next time because if I find it I won't just write in it." He puts his cigarette down, bends over, and squats. He makes numerous pooty noises with his hand and mouth.

He's telling the truth. If he wrote in my book he would definitely brag about it.

I write:

OKAY, IF SOMEONE IS WRITING IN THIS BOOK, KNOW THAT I WILL FIND YOU AND PROSECUTE YOU TO THE FULLEST EXTENT OF THE LAW!!

I WILL ALSO TELL YOUR PARENTS.

TEN

THERE'S A STORAGE bin no one ever uses behind Happy Forest. Perfect for hiding a notebook in. I stash mine there and on my walk back a tiny twig plinks me on the head. I look up and see a robin building a nest. I watch as she drops twigs from her beak and arranges them into a bed on a branch. She fusses with the twigs until satisfied, then flies off for more.

In a few minutes she's back, this time with dead grass. I pull up a toadstool to watch. She studies her twig arrangement thoughtfully.

Then pushes the twigs off the branch.

She drops the grass from her beak and starts to make a whole new nest. Reminds me of the time Mom couldn't decide on a color for the dining room. She had the painter redo it around ten times. He wanted to kill her when she finally went with wallpaper.

I jog to the break area to get my camera. I bump into Hank and tell him about the robin.

"Why not rig up a self-timer?" he suggests. "You can take shots of the bird's progress and don't even have to be there." Genius. We grab an extra Polaroid camera from Lost and Found and head back. He sets up a fixed stand. He mounts the camera to it, rigs a timer, and aims it at the nest.

"What do you think," he says. "A picture every fifteen minutes?"

The robin returns. She's back to twigs. She eyes her grassy nest. Then angrily kicks away the grass and starts over with the twigs. A real waffler, this one.

"Better make it every five minutes," I say. "This cuckoo's cuckoo."

Hank attaches an external jumbo pack of film that he says should last for hours.

CLICK! It spits out the first photo. It's working.

“This is great Hank. Thanks. I hope you never leave Fairy Tale Place.”

“What, and get out of show business?” he says.

Next break I return to the bin, take out my book, and sit on a toadstool. A worm inches over my shoe. I uncap a pen.

MOMS ARE NOT ALWAYS RIGHT

by AUGIE HOBBLE

WILLY THE WORM WAS LAZY.

HE STAYED IN BED ALL DAY.

FOR A WORM, HE WAS A REAL SLUG.

HIS MOM HAD A FAVORITE SAYING.
SHE LIKED TO SAY, "EARLY TO RISE MAKES
WILLY HEALTHY, WEALTHY AND WISE."

"I'LL RISE AND GO GET WEALTHY, IF IT'LL GET HER OFF MY BACK," THOUGHT WILLY. (ACTUALLY WILLY DIDN'T HAVE A BACK BUT HE WIGGLED FROM BED AND OUT THE DOOR ANYWAY.)

UNFORTUNATELY FOR WILLY, ROBIN'S MOM NEXT DOOR HAD A FAVORITE SAYING TOO. SHE TOLD HER LAZY DAUGHTER . . .

"THE EARLY BIRD GETS THE WORM!"

I close my book.

I'm freaking out a little. I still do not have one killer idea. These stories aren't enough and my photo essay is going nowhere. I stuff my notebook in my book bag and head for home thinking this nightmare of a project is going to give me nightmares.

That night I have a nightmare.

It is the dead of night. I'm in the school cafeteria where monster boys and ghoulish girls dine on horrific specials: Eyeballs with Worms. Guts Parmesan. Chicken Fingers. Human Fingers.

"There's a hair in my soup," says a zombie girl.

A lunch lady saunters over and says, "Things are tough all over."

"A single hair?" complains the student, pointing to the soup. "C'mon. This soup's got no taste."

The lunch lady grabs a handful of hairs and throws it into the kid's bowl. "All you kids overseason your food. If it's not extra blood or extra hair, it's extra scabs. And the sodium! Don't even get me started."

I slip out to peek in my Creative Arts class. The chalkboard says:

PROJECTS
YOUR TIME IS UP

There is a single hooded person standing in the corner of the empty class. Is it the Grim Reaper? He pulls back the hood, exposing a severed neck. "What's the matter? Can't get ahead on your project?" says a voice from under his arm. I look down to the head he's carrying. "A head. Get it?" he says. It's that hoodie guy from the park. He laughs crazily, "Ha, ha, ha, ha, ha." I run away. I run through the woods, first on two feet, then on all fours. I growl. I howl. I chase small critters and rip them apart as I devour their bits. From out of nowhere Hogg Wills steps in front of me and I eat him. Whole hog.

Next morning I wake covered in sweat. I kick off soaked sheets and roll over to the open window, sucking in what little breeze there is. I hop out of bed and drag a chair to the closet where I stand on tiptoes to reach the top shelf. I dig under five winter sweaters, a stack of old comic books, and a broken Wii to get to a game of *Sorry*. I lift the box lid, then the game board with all the cards and pieces and stuff to pull my notebook from my "at home" top secret hiding spot. *Heh, heh, excellent hiding place,* I think as I open the book.

My knees turn to rubber. What is this? A beheaded cat?

How?

No.

Not possible. No one could have gotten in here. No one could have found this book. The blood rushes to my head. Feeling overwhelmed. Now voices. I'm hearing voices in my head.

Wait, no, the voices are coming from down the hall. Two voices. Like primeval beasts. Coming from my parents' bathroom. Their words are slow and clumsy. I glance at my wolf wall and one clipping in particular catches my eye: *Werewolves Begat Werewolves.* From old-time folklore it tells of how one werewolf makes another and on and on.

I ease down the hall, moving closer to the strange voices. I put my ear against the door.

"Yoo aw killween me." It is Dad.

"Saw-wee." It is Mom.

"Yoo aw awways in ma waaay . . ."

Did I turn into something last night and then turn *them* into something? I pick up the heavy vase from the hall table.

Just in case. I put it down. What am I thinking? These are my parents. Do I run? Stay? Yes, stay. I have to know. Just a peek then. I mentally plot my escape route in the event I am chased: down the stairs, through the front door, over the fence to the neighbor with the big dog that likes me but growls at everyone else.

Slowly, carefully, I crack the door. I see Mom and Dad in their matching bathrobes. I push the door open the rest of the way. They are not drooling monsters. They are flossing together.

"Awgee, wee don' knog anymo?" says Mom, talking to my reflection in the mirror.

"Awgee, one uv uth coult haff been on thuh toi-wett," says Dad.

"I'm sorry, I thought maybe I had turned you into . . ."

Dad removes his floss. "What?"

"Nothing," I say. "Sorry."

Mom removes her floss. "Did you move my vase?"

"Sorry," I say again, backing away to my room.

That morning on my bike ride to the park I count seven missing cat posters, three missing dog posters, and one for a missing iguana. Something is definitely going on. On top of all that my skin is breaking out too.

I wish Britt was back from Yellowstone. When I try to talk to Claire she grins and says, "Trust me, you're not turning into anything," which I actually hope is true. I thought it would be cool to be a Super Wolf but I definitely don't want to be a "tortured soul cursed for all eternity." Particularly if that curse ends with a head chopping or a silver bullet to the heart. I tell Claire I hope she's right because if at night I *am* turning into a werewolf and if I revert back again tonight and attack my loved ones—

But she only grins and says, "Revert to. Revert *back* to is redundant."

"Can we not correct me for two minutes?" I say, showing her the scribbly pages in my notebook. "And how do you explain these?"

"I do sense something out of the ordinary in these ... but they're not ... Listen, I know you wish you were special, that you could somehow change and take on all the jerks and bullies of the world, but look at me, I have a gift and guess what? My life is still complicated."

What a drama queen. Oughta be on the Storybook Stage.

"We all want to be someone else," she continues. "I'm sure you sometimes wish you weren't you."

"Of*ten*. That's not what I'm talking about. These scribbles ..."

"You need to talk to someone smarter than me about those scribbles."

"Oala?"

"A psychiatrist. Has it been two minutes?"

"Yes."

She gives me her know-it-all smile. "Properly speaking, you shouldn't pronounce the 't' in 'often.'"

I knock on Dad's office door and stick my head in.

"Augie," he says. "Back to knocking I see." Before I can apologize again about this morning he turns serious. "Wait, what broke? Is a Route 66 jalopy down again?"

"No, everything's fine," I say.

"BravO!"

"I was hoping I could check something on your computer."

"Charlotte's (Worldwide) Web too far a walk?"

"I need to print something too."

"Come on in," he says, turning on the printer. "Knock yourself out." He pats my back and heads out into the park.

I look up Moonflower and print out a couple of pages of the trumpet-shaped white flowers. Before I put the computer to sleep I check email. Nothing from Britt in the last few days. He must be having one heck of a time in Yellowstone.

I search around the Magic Tee House, our miniature golf course that's overrun with weeds. I compare the printouts to every white flower and weed I see until I find a match. Moonflower. I gather a "bouquet" and start to leave when I bump into Juliana.

"For me?" she jokes.

"Um, perchance I mighteth spare but one—"

"Hey, take it down a notch. There's no guests around, Augie."

"Right, ha, ha," I say.

Her phone vibrates and she begins answering a text. She walks backstage with her head in her phone, our conversation over.

That night after dinner I tell Mom I'm pretty bushed and hitting the sack early. I grab some pie and head to my room. I lock myself in and barricade the window. I open my backpack. I remove my Moonflower plants and scatter them around my room. I have to be sure once and for all about what might be happening with me. It's going to be a long night. I have books for when I get bored, I have water for when I am thirsty, I have pie for when I want pie. I sit at my computer. I start my rickety old webcam. I tap it a couple of times to get it going, the record light flickers on, and I sit back and wait.

The morning sun wakes me.

Stuffy in here. Window still latched shut, door still locked. I sit up in my chair. Then I see my reflection in the dark computer screen. My face and shirt, covered in red. Red everywhere. *Oh my God. What have I done?* I tap the keyboard, waking my screen from sleep. I fast-forward through my webcam recording. I see myself from last night. I see my eyes droop then close. I see me fall asleep. I watch as

webcam 1
09:03:36 PM
webcam 1
09:47:55
webcam 1
11:14:01 PM
webcam 1
12:05:25
webcam 1
01:11:46 AM
webcam 1
01:52:03

I toss and turn in my chair. I see me scratch my cheek in my sleep, getting red on it. I roll over in my chair and the cherry pie on my stomach falls to the floor. My hands, covered in red cherries, brush against my white shirt. I itch my nose and get more red on me. I touch my collar. More red. I get it everywhere. I fast-forward through about five hours of this before my webcam pooped out at around the 2 a.m. mark. Mom's gonna kill me for ruining this shirt.

Okay, maybe Claire was right. It's a relief to know I'm not some kind of creature. I start to feel better and the idea for a cherry pie horror story begins to form in my brain. "The Pits and the Pendulum" I'll call it. I pull back my rug and lift a floorboard; my new top secret hiding place. I bring up my notebook. I sit at my desk and sharpen a pencil as silly werewolf thoughts are replaced by killer cherry pit ideas. I open my book and almost wet myself.

ronn runneen
runn runn

muss thinkstrat

losst alwaaz
Blak

moov
move Throo A dark

Throu a fog

Tri tRyeen Try Togit

git bak to

One gol goaL

passSs Othurs go opsit WAY

Me go againsT hemm

Fite againsst fITE

2 2 get bAK

bak T oooooooo

to 2 too

back retern

~~feetr~~ reetern 2 awgee re

retern retern too a wgee

bull bulbol

retern to

retern to

muss

reetern to awgee hobbul

My hands are shaking as I clutch the book to my chest.

ELEVEN

THAT DAY AT work my brain is working overtime. *Return to Augie Hobble.* Return to me. Mind going a mile a minute all day long and still going on the bike ride home. Return to me from someone else? Some*thing* else? As I pull into my garage I am surprised to see Britt's family's car in their drive. Back early from Yellowstone. I come through the front door and Mom greets me with a big bear hug, but I slip away to run upstairs. Britt's back! Excellent. Finally, someone I can talk to about the scribbles who won't just make fun.

"Augie?" calls Mom from the foot of the stairs.

"Just a sec," I say.

"Sweetie, I need to talk to you," she says.

I quickly check email to see if Britt has written. Nothing again. I come back downstairs and ask Mom if Britt's called. She tries to give me another hug. He's probably avoiding me because he forgot to bring me a present. "He's probably in his backyard now gathering up some 'Yellowstone Rocks,'" I tell Mom. I smell my favorite meal cooking, beef stroganoff, the one with the onion soup mix and sour cream. "Remember that time they went to Orlando? He brought me a pencil sharpener shaped like Florida. There was an airport receipt at the bottom of the bag. Bought it on his way out of town."

"Augie . . ." Mom says.

"At least after that trip he didn't act all different. Remember that time his family went to England? He came back adding *u*'s to all his words. You'd read an email and it'd be like, 'isn't orange a smashing C-O-L-O-*U*-R?'" I say spelling out the word. "Or 'my jokes are full of much H-U-M-O-*U*-R.' What a M-O-R-O-*U*-N."

"Augie, the Fairweathers are back early because there was an accident. Britt got sick, honey."

I see for the first time Mom's eyes are all red. She asks me to sit with her on the couch. I do. She tears up.

"Augie sweetie, things happen sometimes to people we love and there's no reason why, they simply happen. It's really... really unfair."

Then Dad walks in the door. He never comes home this early. He kisses Mom on the cheek and joins us on the couch.

"Did you ..."

"I was just starting," Mom tells him.

Dad squeezes my shoulder and gives me big puppy dog eyes. What's going on here? Mom begins again but chokes up and can't talk.

"Son," says Dad, taking over. "Britt ... Britt died."

Wait, back up. What?

Can't breathe.

I feel like throwing up. Sometimes Dad uses figures of speech like when he says "we got killed today at the park," but the way he said "Britt died," in that quiet voice, I know he wasn't using any figure of speech.

I throw up after all.

I throw up all over the side of the couch and don't even get yelled at.

"People don't die from allergic reactions," I cry.

"They do, honey. They do. I'm so sorry," says Mom.

"They get really sick or they break out in spots or their face swells up or . . ."

"I'm sorry buddy," says Dad.

We look out the window at Britt's house. The shades are drawn.

"The funeral is Friday. You don't have to go," says Mom.

"It's all right if you don't go," says Dad.

"Everyone will understand," says Mom.

I go.

I wish I hadn't. I watched a talk show once where the experts kept going on about closure this and closure that, but let me tell you, it's not true. I can't get the image of Britt in that super-shiny coffin with those satin cushions out of my head.

I find this photo and leave it on the Fairweathers' doorstep.

I don’t do much of anything for a week.

TWELVE

HE WAS HERE and then he was gone. It's so not real. I see funny cat videos and want to forward them to him. His email address is still here but he's not. It's not right.

Last night he was in my dream. I was at Fairy Tale Place in Birthday Town. I looked to where the big birthday cake sculpture should've been, but instead there was only black. An emptiness, as if the world just dropped off there. From the gloom, I saw a single light. It came closer and closer until I saw it was Britt holding a candle, an old-time candle like you see in storybook pictures. He was trying to get to where I was, but he couldn't. He couldn't get from the black into the light. "How do I get to the other side?" he yelled to me. I didn't know what he meant. I yelled back, "You're already on the other side."

Then I woke up.

I was probably dreaming of this because of that mural idea I had. I don't know.

Every Tuesday Mom picks up Grandpa and brings him by for a visit. He's kinda forgetful and all he ever wants to do is rock on the porch swing. He brought a watermelon for us this Tuesday, but I don't feel like eating. He nibbles at it, spitting the seeds onto our rock lawn.

"Grandpa, what do you think happens after we die?"

"Oh, I don't know," he says. "You rest."

"Are you afraid of it?"

"My grandson Augie is afraid of pigeons."

"*I'm* Augie, Grandpa."

He pulls a shaker out of his pocket and salts his melon.

"Do you know what a late checkout is, Andy? One time, I'm going back maybe forty, forty-five years, I found myself a guest of El Rancho Royale. Business trip. Remember when I peddled them novelty doo-dads?"

"Uh-uh."

"No matter. So, El Rancho, fine hotel. Albuquerque's finest. Crystal chandeliers, indoor pool. Pretty. Boy, I was et up with it. When that noon checkout rolled around, I couldn't hardly leave. I called down to the front desk and inquired about what they call a 'late checkout.' Got me an extra two hours. Spent it soaking in the tub, sipping RC Cola from the minibar, and looking up at all the crystal in those chandeliers.

"Late checkout. I'm gonna try one of them deals when my number's up here. Talk to the Big Guy. See if I can't get a couple extra years." He ricochets a seed off Mom's porch bell, *ping!* "Life's a lulu, Arnie. Enjoy it."

"Lately, I'm finding it hard finding much to enjoy."

"This watermelon ain't bad," he says.

First day back to work.

Fairy Tale Place is like a safe house to me. A big striped and polka-dotted safe house. I pass through its walls and for the most part the real world doesn't follow. Outside I hear a bus driver yelling. I hear a jackhammer. I hear motorcycles revving their engines. In here, the sound of glockenspiels.

It's 3 p.m. The SANTAstic Show is starting under the oversize chimney. Sharon Jean and Wanda Jean sing "The Twelve Days of Christmas." Despite the dancing reindeer and twinkly music, I get choked up. It seems like yesterday Britt was here counting the birds in this song.

"Ho, ho, ho, peace and joy to all!" says Santa, emerging from the chimney to hand out cheap little cellophaned candy canes and cheaper jokes. "Frosty!" he says, spotting a beverage puddle. "I pleaded with you to stay out of the sun!" The guests chuckle.

The obnoxious teenagers from a few weeks ago, the one with the Route 666 T-shirt and his whiskered friend, are back. They lean against the Polar Express-o coffee caboose.

"My, you are the tallest elves Santa's ever seen!" Santa says, winking at them.

"You're the fattest elf we've ever seen," says Route 666.

"Maybe you should lay off the fruitcake, Fruitcake," says Chin-whiskers.

"Gentlemen, I plead guilty," says Santa, rubbing his belly. "Mrs. Claus does indulge ol' Santa."

"The Mrs.? Her fault? She's the enabler?"

Santa frowns, gives them candy canes, and moves on. They follow.

"You know, I never got that ATV I asked for," says Route 666. "Or the trampoline. Or the pump air rifle with the scope."

Santa tries to play along. "That's a lot to fit in Santa's sleigh."

"Or the rabbit trap, or the *Dora the Explorer* phone."

His friend shoots him a look.

"It's a cool phone," he says.

"How about you boys move along now?" says Santa.

Chin-whiskers grabs Santa's cap and throws it to 666.

A woman pushing a stroller says, "Excuse me? I believe we were here first."

Santa is helpless as they play catch over his head.

A father tells his son, "Kyle, you're missing some good shots here. Where's your camera?"

Juliana wanders over from Enchanted Castle.

I step up to the troublemakers. "C'mon guys," I whisper.

They do a little basketball skirmish; 666 tosses the hat back to Chin-whiskers who runs past Santa, giving his beard a little tug before slam-dunking the cap into a fiberglass stocking.

The guests boo.

"C'mon guys," I say, "be cool."

Whiskers says, "*You* be cool, trash boy."

There's a half-empty soda cup on top of a trash bin. Whiskers pours it on my head. "Cool now?"

"Yeah, cool now trash boy?" says his friend as they hop a fence out of the park.

Santa retrieves his cap from the stocking, then turns to the crowd with a great big Santa smile. "Ho, ho, ho! I know two little boys who may just make Santa's Naughty List this year. Now, who wants a candy cane?"

The crowd laughs.

Humiliated, I slump away, a wet trail of pop behind me.

I drag my sorry self down Pork Avenue. I stop at the third little pig's house. The house of bricks. I go inside. Dark and safe. I pull the door shut. I put my pan and broom down and crouch, licking at the pop like blood from a wounded paw. A guest peeks in the window and tries the locked door. I back against the wall and into the fake fireplace. There's a wolf tail dangling from a cauldron. I unhook it. I pin it to the back of my pants. I check myself in the funhouse mirror. I retreat to a dark corner, circle twice, curl into a ball, and close my eyes.

I dream. In my dream as in life I have drawn the short straw. I am not superhero strong. I do not leap through the air and save damsels in distress or conquer bad guys.

I do not save my best friend. I am a wolf scavenging for scraps. I am a wolf chasing small mice and voles. I travel in a straight line. I howl at the moon but not in a scary way. Mournful, you would say. I mark my territory with my pee. When I hook up with a pack my wolf self is not that different from my human self. I am timid. I am weak. I am the loner of the group. I do not have a mate. I am not the alpha male. Not even beta. I am the low-ranking omega, the one picked on by the rest of the pack.

"Hey buddy," says Dad from outside the brick house. "Hank said I might find you in here. Everything okay?"

I open an eye.

"There's a corn dog out here with your name on it."

I sniff in the direction of the window.

"I know your mother says only veggies before supper, but with all due respect, corn? Vegetable, heh, heh."

I stay in the corner.

"Maybe later," he says and I hear him leave the corn dog on the windowsill and walk away, his keys jangling down Pork Avenue.

There are no superheroes in real life. No make-believe. No happily ever after. Just death and lowly omegas. The scribbles in my notebook? Just scribbles. Who am I kidding? Too much sugar. The hairs on my chin and hands? What health class calls "the awkward stage." I come out of my brick house "den." I move through the park in a straight line, my head down. The lowly omega. I sniff at planters and food wrappers. My wolf tail drags behind me, collecting popcorn and gum.

I stop and mark my territory behind a concrete mushroom.

I walk through fake woods to real woods to scavenge for blackberries where I stumble on a camera and tripod. On the ground I see a pile of Polaroids in the dirt. I pause. I had forgotten about the robin's nest and the self-timer.

Two birds. Two. I thought it was one picky bird, but all robins look alike and two are fighting over the same nest site. I shove the pictures in my pocket and forage under a bush. A bug crawls up my arm. I nip. Missed it. Nip again. Got it. I eat blackberries. Spit out seeds. I circle twice and lie under the shade of a tree. There's whimpering. It's me. Didn't realize I was doing it.

I wipe my eyes. I head back. I walk until the real trees of birch and oak become fiberglass and plastic again.

"Did you get my card?" says a voice. It's Claire from behind her Sippee cart.

I don't answer.

"I'm so sorry about your friend."

Couldn't she have foreseen Britt's death and prevented it in some way?

"I like your tail," she says.

I pick at a wad of gum in the fur.

She says, "Peanut butter works best for removing—" She stops. "Wait. Something is about to happen."

I listen but hear only the familiar sounds of Fairy Tale Place: the calliope, the electronic beeps and boops from the Hunger Video Games arcade.

Then I hear it. Shouting.

Two male guests. They are yelling and chasing a third person, a girl, up Jack 'n' Jill's hill. The girl's dress whips behind her as she sprints ahead of them. The girl makes it to the wishing well. She moves left, then right with the men mirroring her movements on the opposite side of the well. One gets too close and she beans him with Jack's pail of water.

He topples down the hill. A guest says, "Ha, she broke Jack's crown!" He rolls into the entrance gate of Hairy Potter's Petting Zoo. I look down and see his black socks and sandals. It's that snoop from Mom's shop. Now I recognize the girl on top of the hill too: the Gypsy's daughter Nicoletta.

"Shouldn't you help?" Claire says.

And get pop poured on me again? Uh-uh.

The man on the hill finally corners Nicoletta and handcuffs her. He drags her down kicking and yelling.

"Bullies," says a guest.

"Varmints," says Cowboy Roy joining the small crowd.

Dad arrives and makes a big show of demanding an explanation. He whips out his phone to dial security, but the man in the black socks and sandals stands and like in Mom's shop flashes a very big, very intimidating agent badge of some kind and Dad, always mindful of bad publicity, backs down.

"You okay Nicoletta?" says Cowboy Roy.

The other agent pulls her hair. A wig, it comes off in his hand. "More like Nick," he says.

Before anyone can ask why Nicoletta is actually a boy in disguise, Zeb the bull who has been working the broken petting zoo gate butts it to the ground. Animals are suddenly running every which way.

"Stampede!" yells Cowboy Roy as a tiny chick runs over his boot. Livestock is scurrying past park guests and over flower bushes. The agent in the sandals is blindsided by a pygmy goat and goes down again. Ol' Paint, Cowboy Roy's horse, rears up on her hindquarters like they do in the movies. The other agent jumps back from her, and Nicoletta, seizing the distraction, breaks free of the agent and steps to the other side of Ol' Paint. Nicoletta, with hands cuffed behind her—*his*—back, bounds up bales of hay like stairs. He scrambles onto Ol' Paint's back and Ol' Paint bolts. She gallops straight down Lilliput Lane, hopping Humpty Dumpty's wall and sending the concrete Humpty crashing to the pavement. He breaks into hundreds of pieces. No king's horses or king's men will be putting that eggman together again.

"Yee-haw!" says Claire. "Go, Paint. Go!"

"Hey, that's ma horse," yells Roy. "Stop, Paint. Stop!"

Roy hops on Bessie the mule, interrupting her free snack of spilled popcorn. He spurs her sides. *Hee-haw*, she brays. She kicks twice, then trots in the direction of Ol' Paint.

Dad and the other hosts scramble trying to corral the animals as the two agents hop a fence to get to their car. They pass Oala sitting on a toadstool in the center of the mayhem. She has her head in her hands as she mumbles Gypsy curses. I hear her put a curse on the agents' teeth. Curses all their teeth to fall out. All but one for each agent, which she curses with a toothache.

"I think that would qualify as a 'once-in-a-lifetime theme park experience,'" Claire says, quoting Dad's BravO rule.

A pig tries to run through her legs. She puts her arms around its neck.

"He was hiding something," she says. She closes her eyes to concentrate. "Nick is not what he seems."

"Well, he's not a she," I mumble.

"Uh-uh, something else. It's not clear yet but Nick, Nicoletta, whatever you want to call him, is hiding a dark secret. I see . . . I see . . ." She shakes her head no. Nothing coming to her. She opens her eyes. "I do however see a goat swallowing your tail."

I turn. There is a goat chewing my fake wolf tail. I nudge him and he ambles away, taking the tail with him. Claire wrestles the pig back into her pen. I round up the emu and some other animals. I catch Macaw-ly Culkin and return him to his perch. As I close his cage door I notice the newspaper on the bottom of his cage and the familiar face looking up at me.

Back in the brick house I sit holding the week-old newspaper.

Britt.

It's Britt's obituary. It reads:

Fairweather

Britt Fairweather

Britt Fairweather left this earth much too soon when he passed away while vacationing with family at Yellowstone National Park. The cause of death was allergic reaction to peanuts which

Beloved mot
grandmother
by her son,
Monroe, d
Ralston of
Ralston o
and daug
of Oxfor
Meury o
Eleanor
She was
of Lauren
Neil Rals
of Fairfi
of Coven
of Monr
After gr
High Sc
Ralston
began
house
of thei
There

I stop.

My hands begin to tremble.

No one told me it was peanuts.

The cookie.

I had slipped a cookie into Britt's bag. It was before his family left for Yellowstone. I thought it would be a nice surprise for the back of the car. Who doesn't like a surprise cookie? But I know I checked that cookie. I'm careful. I knew Britt had allergies.

I slip into Charlotte's (Worldwide) Web and log on to the Mendoza's Bakery site. I find the cookie: El Bomba. Right, just as I remembered: Ingredients: *cacao*, that's gotta be cocoa. *Azucar*, sugar, right? *Sal*, salt. *Vainilla*, vanilla. *Cacahuate* . . . caw-caw-hoo-ah-tey. *Caca* has to be a chocolate something or other . . . cocoa powder maybe.

I go to a Spanish to English site. I type in "cacahuate."

The translation appears: "peanut."

No.

Not right. Salt is *sal*! Cocoa is *cacao*! Peanut should be *peanuté* not *cacahuate*!

I stumble back to my brick house.

My brain in a fog.

Nothing making sense.

Britt. It's one thing to lose your best friend—but to be the responsible party. The irresponsible party.

I curl up in the dark corner. The tears come. I bury my face in the dirt floor. No, no, no, no, no, no, no. Dirt and tears then mud. Britt. I make my body a tight ball. Something stabs my leg. A sharp corner from the robin's nest Polaroids in my pocket. I toss them to the floor. I pull my hair down over my eyes. I claw at the dirt. My hand tightens on a stone. I sit up. I wind my arm back and face the mirror. I stare at my distorted face in the funhouse glass. I start to throw the stone but stop when I see one of the Polaroids enlarged in a ripple of the glass. It shows a figure behind the robin's nest. I squint, trying to make out details. I snatch the picture and run with it to Dad's office. I blow it up on the Xerox machine.

Britt would be laughing now. The fuzzy image looks exactly like the pictures in his *Mysterious Sightings* book. Except this one is not Bigfoot or Nessie. This one is a werewolf. And this werewolf is wearing Nicoletta's troll doll necklace.

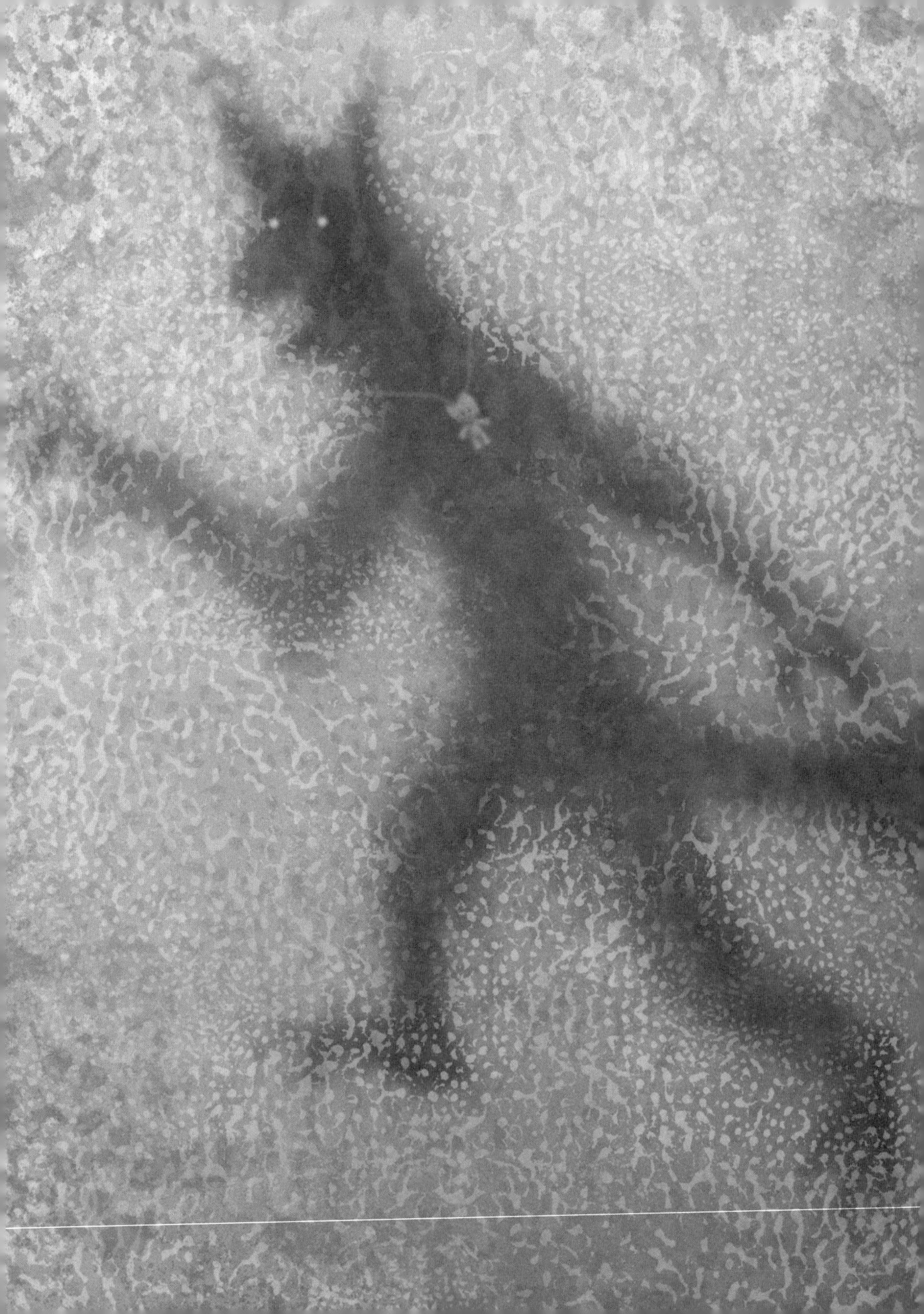

I know what I have to do.

A tortured soul cursed for all eternity. I've got to find Nicoletta/Nick and take it all the way. I'll make it right. I deserve no less. Britt deserves no less.

I leave a note on Dad's office desk. I fill a water bottle and hop on my bike. Tire's dead. I reach for a pump but something better catches my eye.

I ease the tiny Dustbowl Adventure jalopy out of the garage. I push it through the back gate and, when out of earshot, start it up and drive out through the North Woods and into the miles of desert beyond.

I putt-putt-putt through dusty plains. I swerve to avoid big rocks and once, a big snake. It's a good thing the dust bowl jalopy was modified to handle large amounts of dust. I am one big cloud of it.

The land is flat and still except for the little dust devils that dance on the horizon. Out here the colors are sepia like in the first part of *The Wizard of Oz*. That Oz twister is still the best I've ever seen in a movie. Better than in the new CG movies. Britt always said it was just a big sock some effects guys were spinning. It was a good one though.

In spite of its toylike appearance the jalopy is pretty durable. Britt and I used to play bumper cars in these. We weren't supposed to. Did anyway. Good mileage too. I stop only once after an hour or so to add gas from the can in the trunk.

I feel free. Everything clear now.

I step on the gas.

THIRTEEN

A-OOOO-GA! I honk the old-timey horn. There's a mule in my way and I can't get around her on account of Rual Jessup's barn on the right and a broken-down tractor on the left. It's true what they say about mules being stubborn. She won't budge. I get out of my little car. I recognize the marking on her side. I always thought it looked a little like a pancake with ears. "Hey Bess," I say. "Where's Roy, girl?"

Dr. Jessup's head pops out from the hayloft. "That you Augie?"

I know Dr. Jessup from the park. He's a vet who comes twice a year to check on our animals. The rest of the time he's out here alone in the middle of nowhere.

"It's me, sir. Cowboy Roy here?"

"Was, 'bout two hours back. Left Bessie with me. She saw that basket of carrots." He chuckles thinking about it. "Wouldn't walk another step. Ate half the basket before Roy and me could stop her."

"Sorry. We'll pay for the carrots."

"Naw, I got plenty. Hold on. You just reminded me of something." I hear him jogging down the barn stairs. He joins me in the road. "Aug," he says, "hear the one about the mule and preacher?"

"I'm in kind of a hurry."

"I'll make it quick. Seems there was this guy." He's telling me anyway. "Bought a mule from a preacher. Now this guy was told by the preacher that the mule had been trained in a very special way; the only way to make the mule walk was to say 'Hallelujah' and the only way to make him stop was to say 'Amen.'"

"Was Roy on foot?"

"Naw, I lent him Crackerjack. Now listen up. The guy tried out the preacher's instructions: 'Hallelujah!' he said. Sure enough the mule began to trot. 'Amen!' he said. Sure enough the mule stopped."

I tug on Bessie's bridle. She won't budge.

"So with a 'Hallelujah,' off rode this guy for the hills."

"Which way did he go?"

"The hills! The hills! You not listening?"

"I meant Roy."

"Oh, Roy. Headed north." Dr. Jessup takes Bessie's bridle and leads her with a carrot to the barn. "Anyways, the guy rides through the hills until he comes upon a cliff, but he'd been traveling so long seems he forgot the word to make the mule stop. 'Whoa!' he said, 'Halt!' he said. But that mule just kept on a' going. 'Stop!' he said. 'Cease!' he said, but that mule trotted faster and faster toward that cliff. Finally, in desperation, the guy says a prayer. 'Please, dear Lord. Please make this mule stop before I go off the end of this cliff, please, oh please, oh please, in all that's holy, AMEN!' Well, upon hearing Amen wouldn't you know that mule came to an abrupt stop just one inch short of the edge of that cliff? You can imagine the fellow's relief. He let out a big ol' sigh . . . 'HALLELUJAH!' he said."

Dr. Jessup makes a wide grin, tickled with himself. "Git it?"

"Hallelujah," I say. "Oh yeah. I get it. Pretty good one."

Dr. Jessup holds up a pair of sawed-off handcuffs. "Found these bracelets in the barn."

"Nick!"

"Now that was Roy's conclusion as well."

"Which way'd Nick go? Along old 66?"

"Ruint my new hand saw."

"Dr. Jessup, was he following old 66?"

He points to hoofprints in the sand.

"Appears so."

Another hour of traveling at full speed and I catch up with Roy. He and Crackerjack are following the old, abandoned Route 66 highway.

"Augie. How-do? You come all this way to find me?"

"Actually, I'm looking for Nick."

"That makes for two of us, pard."

The jalopy sputters and steams.

"I admire your mode of transport," Roy says as he unties his bandana and uses it to loosen the red-hot radiator cap. It spits and whistles then *PHWEEEEEEEEEEeeeeeeew* . . . the jalopy shuts down.

"I think ya kilt it Augie. Vehicular homicide."

We push the jalopy into some brush and cover it with tumbleweeds. Roy pulls me up on Crackerjack to ride behind him.

"I saw a helicopter a while ago," I say.

"I saw one too."

"Figure it's those agents?"

"Yup. Your folks know you're gone?"

"I left a note."

"You're gonna catch heck. Best call next phone we come across."

"You don't have a cell?"

He shakes his head. "Cowboy don't use a cell." He says this like it's universally understood. "Nick owe you money or something?" Roy asks.

"Something," I say.

Stars appear in the blue evening sky looking like twinkle lights from the park. We arrive at an abandoned gas station. Roy says it was once the type of place that sold beef jerky and trucker tapes by singers named Red. Like many Route 66 stops, it had an attraction. Its sign reads HOOT AT AL.

I'm wondering who Al is when I see a yellowed flyer stuck on a barb wire fence.

HOOT AT AL

Some of the letters must've fallen off over the years.

SHOOTOUT AT THE O.K. CORRAL

Old-time saloon doors creak as we pass through them to a run-down shooting gallery. Roy picks up one of the toy guns, the cord connecting it to the counter falling apart in his hands. He blows off the dust. "You varmints been causin' a heap of trouble in Dodge. Go on now, slap leather." Roy draws. "Pow!" he says, pointing his six-shooter at a plywood Sam Hall. At Billy the Kid, "Pow! Pow!" At Jesse James, "Pow!" At Fievel from *Fievel Goes West* grouped without reason with these dangerous desperadoes. "Eat lead, cartoon mouse! Pow! Pow! Pow!"

"We need to get going," I remind Roy. But he tells me it's too dark now for tracking so we might as well set up camp. We walk around back to the long-closed Flaming Arrow Tepee Motel. But after getting a whiff inside a concrete tepee, we think it best to camp under the stars "cowboy-style" as Roy calls it.

He tells me to make a fire. I try feebly rubbing two sticks together then banging rocks but get nothing. I don't know the first thing about fire making. Above, the old billboard advertising the Flaming Arrow sways with the wind. I shake its base and a big chunk of the sign falls to my feet. It's the section with the painted flames. I throw it into my pit and Roy tosses a match on it, turning the painted fire into real fire.

Roy sits beside me and eases some cans into the pit. He sings:

"There was blood on the saddle, and blood all around,

And a great big puddle, of blood on the ground.

"Tex Ritter," he says. "You could do a lot worse than ol' Tex. Know him?"

"Not really."

"Oh pity the cowboy, all bloody and dead,

A bronco fell on him and mashed in his head."

He hands me a can. "Eat up."

I look at the label: asparagus tips.

"Dr. Jessup was out of beans," he says.

I make a face.

"You can have my Brussels sprouts if you prefer."

I prefer to keep looking for Nick. But I guess we have to call it a night. I spread out on the ground and close my eyes.

"First light, Augie. Time to hit the trail," says Roy next morning.

Roy hands me a can of broccoli rabe he warmed on the embers of the fire.

"Way I figure," he says, "Nick's headed for the caves at Dante's Point."

I eat a spoonful. "Dante's Point? Did you study the tracks in the sand?" I ask, trying to distract myself from the taste in my mouth. "Did you find a clue? A swatch of clothing on some brush?"

"Naw, it's just Ol' Paint *always* heads to Dante's Point. She's like a big ol' puppy dog dragging her owner to the dog park. There's cactus fruit there. She loves it. I'm sure Nick will try to steer her otherwise but eventually he'll give up. Anyways, that's not a bad hideout for a fugitive on the lam. It'll take a posse a good while to track him there."

Even with a "hat" made from yucca leaves, my nose and cheeks burn red from the morning sun. I forgot my Chap-Stick and feel naked without it. The insides of my legs ache from Crackerjack's swaying and his bony back does my butt no favors. I could holler. I know now why movie cowboys are always yodeling.

A few miles later Roy nods to two towering rock formations. They look like twin horns. "Dante's Point," says Roy. We hear a whinny and there's Ol' Paint feeding on cactus fruit just like Roy predicted. A few steps away is Nick, eyes closed and covered in sweat. His leg is twisted at an unnatural angle.

"Nick," calls Roy.

He doesn't move.

Roy shakes him gently. "Nick," he says. "Nicoletta."

His eyes open.

Roy gives him his canteen.

"I think I have broke my leg," says Nick.

"Yup."

"Stupid horse does not like strangers to ride her."

Roy stands and pats Ol' Paint's snout. "That's right. Good girl," he says. He gives her a kiss. "You know in the Old West they'd hang a man for horse thievery."

Nick takes a sip of water. "Same penalty for woman?"

Roy smiles. "We'll talk about that petticoat later. For now we need to get you and that leg to a hospital."

Nick shakes his head.

"You can't just sit here."

"Moonflower," Nick says. "Did you see any?"

"Moonflower? What's that, Gypsy remedy?"

"I know what it is," I say.

"You need to find Moonflower," says Nick. "Lots. Then drag me to it."

We make a bed from branches; Roy calls it a travois. He hitches it to Ol' Paint. Roy then makes a splint from a branch and straps it to Nick's leg using torn pieces from his dress. We help Nick onto the travois and Roy begins walking Ol' Paint, leading her by the reins. I follow behind, walking Crackerjack and talking to Nick.

"When our class studied the Civil War," I say, "we read about boys dressing like girls to hide from the army. You were hiding weren't you?"

He doesn't answer.

"Those agents. They were some kind of special agents?"

He snorts. "*Special* special agents."

"They look for people like you?"

No answer.

"Because of what you are?"

No answer.

"That night in the woods. It was you who attacked me, wasn't it? Because what you did... it didn't take."

He looks at me, puzzled.

"I want it to take," I say.

Roy looks back and I lower my voice. "I read about your kind: tortured souls cursed for all eternity."

"This you want?"

"Yes. Eternal punishment. I have done a terrible thing."

"Terrible like rip out lungs? Eat brains? Hold bloody still-beating heart in hand while now-heartless body falls to your feet? You kill? You kill with fangs? You kill with claws?"

"I kill . . . with cookie."

We're interrupted by Roy. "Y'all sound like a coupla peahens cackling over here." He dismounts and nods to a patch of large white trumpet-shaped flowers. "That it?"

It is. Moonflower. I smell its sickly sweet smell. Sweeter than the chocolate-smelling guest-bait we force out of Charley's Chocolate Factory.

Before we can help Nick off the travois he does it himself, rolling into the flowers. It's early afternoon so the blooms are barely open, but Nick rubs his leg and starts to bend it at the knee.

"Probably best you don't work that leg so much," says Roy.

Nick bends his leg all the way, snapping the splint in half. He works the joint back and forth. The leg bulks up as thick hairs sprout from it.

"Or you can do that. That works," says Roy, pushing his hat to the back of his head and taking a step back. Nick flips over on his belly and rises up on all fours. He raises his hairy head, shaking away his humanity. He rears up on his hind legs growing taller and beefier. He is covered in fur. He lifts his head to the sky and howls. Roy takes a few more steps back, not believing his eyes. Nick turns to him, growling.

"Augie, you couldn'ta told me this might happen?" hollers Roy, whipping out a six-shooter. "Nicky, don't make me use this silver bullet."

Nick trots to him in a straight line and slaps away the toy gun that Roy must've taken from the shooting gallery. Nick throws Roy into the air. Roy slams into an immense formation of Mesozoic rock which, if you had to be tossed into the air by a lycanthrope and had to land on something, would not be your first choice. He slides down the rock like a broken cowboy doll and before he reaches the ground Nick is on him. He thrashes at him with sharp teeth and sharper claws.

"Wolf!" I cry.

Nick turns from Roy to me. He exposes a mouthful of white teeth and I imagine what Moze might say: *My, what big teeth you have, Grandma.*

I step forward, my arms limp at my sides.

I'm ready.

I close my eyes.

I hear the snarling and feel the hot breath.

This is it. The do-over.

I am pushed to the ground violently. A voice in my ear says, "Stay down."

I hear a *WHOOP*, *WHOOP*, *WHOOP*, and open an eye. I see helicopters rising over the big red Mesozoics. I see one of those special special agents pinning me. I see a net drop onto Nick the wolf and half a dozen agents surrounding him.

FOURTEEN

SPECIAL SPECIAL AGENT Edwards, the one with the black socks and sandals, drives me home.

"A simple thank you might be in order," he says.

"For who?"

"For the agent who saved your little heinie from a rabid wolf."

"Wasn't a rabid wolf," I say.

"Looked pretty rabid to me."

"I mean it wasn't a wolf. You know what it was."

"I do. I'll say it again, *rabid* wolf. Been eating all the cats in the area."

"Why couldn't you have left him alone?"

"Not a cat person?"

"You and I both know that wolf was Nick. It's not the first time. He attacked me once before when he was like that."

"Ha! That's a good 'un!" he says. "We found Nick before we ever got to you and that wolf." He pulls off the highway and parks in front of a drab stucco building. "Gotta make a quick stop. Make sure you're hunky-dory." We go through the main entrance and down a hall to a door with one of those security touch pad things. Edwards punches in some numbers and we move on to a kind of lab where a guy in a white coat pricks my finger and smears my blood on a glass microscope slide.

"I'm not really that comfortable with this," I tell Edwards.

"You've never been to the doctor's before?"

"Never one with security touch pads."

The guy in the white coat studies the slide and shakes his head negative to Agent Edwards.

"Congratulations," says Edwards. "Rabies free."

We hear loud foot stomps in a room across the hall and the guy in the white coat elbows the door narrowing my view of what looked like a very tall guy being studied by more people in white coats. I rubberneck, trying to get a better peek through the door crack, when Edwards steps in front of me, pointing to his watch. "Gotta roll," he says.

Then we're back in the car.

"Your folks were pretty relieved you're okay."

"You talked to my parents?"

"We called, sure. Told them not to worry, that you, the cowboy, and 'the apprehended,' Mr. Nick Olgasteiga, were safe and sound. Just a little scare with a rabid wolf."

"Werewolf you mean."

"Right. Your folks told me all about your wolf wall. You're a regular boy who cried werewolf, ain't ya?"

"I know what you guys are. You keep stuff from the public. Aliens and monsters and stuff. I've seen movies like that."

"Movies, huh? Real life ain't no movie, Hobble."

He turns the radio on. Then turns it back off. He kinda goes "pfft" with his mouth, blowing out air like he's suddenly annoyed or something. "You know, I get so tired of every*one* thinking every*thing* they don't understand is some conspiracy. Ever consider some folks might just be working to *better* society? Ever consider that? Not everything is so sinister, son." He turns the radio on. He does that "pfft" thing again and turns the radio back off. "Velcro," he says.

"Velcro?"

"Yes, Velcro. You know how an engineer came up with Velcro? By studying the burrs in his socks. Sonar? Sonar was developed by scientists analyzing the flight patterns of bats. Helicopters hover like what? Dragonflies. It's not a coincidence. Stealth technology for aircraft, ships, etc.? That didn't come from thin air . . ."

"Bigfoot uses a kind of stealth camouflage. I read it. That's why no one ever catches him and . . . *Ah!* that was a bigfoot back there. The tall guy across the hall. You *are* with a secret government agency."

"Why does everything have to be a secret government agency with you?"

"Well, I doubt you're with some hairdo company chasing werewolves as a cure for baldness."

He stares straight ahead for a few seconds, tapping the steering wheel. "Okay, I'll tell you a little secret. Lean in."

I lean in.

"Now don't spread this around," he whispers. "I'm with a big food consortium. Gluten-Free Diet. You've heard of it, right?"

"Of course."

"Our group developed it from studying the dietary habits of the Loch Ness Monster."

"Har, har," I say sarcastically.

"How do you think Nessie's lived so long? Absolutely no breads. No pasta. Eats only seafood."

"You're making fun. I get it."

"Now we're doing the same with wolves. Hope to develop snack cakes made from little bunny rabbits and kitty cats."

"I get it. Your lips are sealed about what you do."

He exhales one last time. "Everyone thinks they know everything."

He turns on the radio. It's playing that old song:

Aahwoo, Werewolves of London, Aahwoooo . . . !

He turns the radio off.

When we get to my house, Mom and Dad are waiting in the driveway.

"Augie how could you have gone off like that?" says Mom.

"And your note: *Went to help Nick. Back soon.* You call that a note?" says Dad.

"Honey, it's admirable you wanting to help Nick, but—"

"But, best we let the proper authorities handle it," says Dad. "The professionals."

"Apparently Nick was a fugitive, Augie," says Mom. "On the lam, as they say. I hope they're not too hard on the poor kid."

"I'm sure it will all work out for the best," says Edwards. He musses up my hair, shakes Dad's hand, and gets back in his car. He tips an imaginary hat to Mom. "Ma'am," he says, then speeds away.

"Thank goodness you're okay," says Mom, walking me back to the house.

"Thank goodness the papers didn't get wind of this. I could see the headline: *Oracle's Offspring O-rrested! Authorities UnAmused With Amusement Park!*" says Dad. "I don't need any bad publicity before our Scary Tale Place opening."

They have no clue. This isn't about a fugitive on the lam. It's crazier than that. It's about a fugitive on *the lamb*. And cat. And human. I could set them straight. Tell them about Nick being a werewolf. But Agent Edwards is right. Who's gonna believe the boy who cries werewolf?

In bed that night I replay the trip in my head. I think about Nick and our weird, weird world. I'll bet he's in some Area 51–type bunker making Moonflower arrangements and scratching fleas. Dad said Oala skipped town and Roy was at County General with a concussion and some busted bones.

"Night, Augie," says Mom, sticking her head in my room. She nods to the door. "Open or closed?"

"Closed," I say.

"I know the last few weeks have been rough on you Augie . . ."

"I'm sorry Mom."

"Well, your father and I have discussed it and we're not going to punish you this time." She looks at me for a long time then turns and closes the door.

But she doesn't understand. I want to be punished.

Next morning I ask Mom where the Fairweathers are as I look out the window to their darkened house.

"Away," says Mom. "With Clara's family in Tulsa."

"Did they say when they'd be back?"

"A few weeks I think."

I write an email.

> TO: FairweatherFamily@sw.com
>
> FROM: HobNob03@sw.com
>
> SUBJECT: urgent
>
> Dear Mr. and Mrs. Fairweather,
> There is something I need to tell you. I want to tell you in person. Please let me know when you return and I will come over.
> Sincerely, Augie

FIFTEEN

CREATIVE ARTS SEEMS so unimportant compared to the big things. Life. Death. The mysteries of our world. Compared to that stuff it must seem ridiculous to worry over an arts project. Still I do. I can't help it. I never told anyone, but the real reason I failed Creative Arts? I choked. It wasn't that my projects were completely awful, they were just, you know, awful enough. Especially after I saw Britt's amazing papier mâché self-portrait. Who can compete with that? So at the last minute I panicked and turned in a blank piece of white cardboard. I called it "Drawing a Blank." I wasn't trying be a wise guy. I really thought it was "conceptual" or something. Tindall thought otherwise. Tindall thought I was trying to be a wise guy. Tindall thought I gave the project no thought at all when in fact I probably put as much thought and time into my ideas as anyone.

They say failure makes you stronger. They say you learn from your mistakes. I find this not to be the case. Failure only makes me sick to my stomach and more nervous for the next time.

And now it's the next time.

My Cinderella story? My mural idea? My crossword song? My sketches? As Britt says, junk, junk, junk, and junk.

Choking. Again.

So what do I do? I spend the day before my due date cutting and pasting robin Polaroids onto a piece of poster board. It's a takeoff on tweeting. See, people tweet but birds were the original tweeters, old school.

BIRD **tweets** DECIPHERED

By AUGIE HOBBLE

TRANSLATION: TWEET. TWEET. TWEET.

When I show it at breakfast Mom says "it's amusing" and Dad says "yes, very amusing" which I know is their polite way of saying "it stinks" and "it really stinks." I start to get that old sick feeling in my stomach. I can't even touch my oatmeal. Gotta rethink this.

I run up to my room and fish under my mattress for my notebook. Stuffed it in there weeks ago. Haven't written in it. Haven't even looked at it in weeks. But I remember some crazy beat poetry Tindall once read to us and I think of my pages with the scribbles on them.

"Augie, you're going to be late," Mom calls from the stairs.

I quickly skim for the pages with the crazy sugar-fueled scribbles.

"Augie, it's eight!"

I tear them out. I write a title, "Wolf Thoughts," and write my name on the first page. I staple the pages together and throw them in my book bag.

I run down the stairs.

"Where's the robin collage?" says Mom.

"Got something better," I say, running out the door.

This could work, I think as I pedal to school. The scribbles are the complete opposite of the minimal "Drawing a Blank." These pages are crammed with stuff. Like weird poetry.

I get to Gerald R. Ford Middle School under a gray sky. I pass through the little kids playground where lonely swings sway in the breeze. I run up the fourteen steps to the front door, down the empty hall, and into Mr. Tindall's class where I drop the pages on his desk. I look up at the clock. Made it. And when I leave the school it's with a not-so-bad feeling for the first time in weeks.

Look at that, the sun is even coming out.

Next day we are due back for our grade. I sit and watch kids receive their work with bright red grades and comments applauding their efforts.

I don't get my project back. I get a note:

> Augie, please see me after class.
> —Mr. Tindall

I figure after suffering through Dewey Webster reciting his 'Oh, the Places Dewey Goes' then Darla Gumm and that wheezing accordion of hers, maybe Tindall wants to congratulate me out of earshot of them. As they file out he finishes erasing the blackboard, then sits on the edge of his desk to face me. He holds my torn pages of crazy scribbling.

"Augie, I'm going to give you a pass on this."

A pass? What happened to a letter grade?

"I also want you to know that I am always here if you need someone to talk to."

He flips through my pages and in a concerned voice asks, "Is there anything you want to tell me? Anything going on at home or . . ."

And it dawns on me my project backfired. He didn't get it. Why did I think it was a good idea? Disaster. My brain is going a mile a minute. I feel like I'm going to explode.

"El Bomba!" I blurt out. I can't believe I said it. It must've been building inside of me for so long it had to get out.

"El Bomba?" he says. *"The bomb?"*

"It's a cookie."

"Oh," he says all disappointed like I'm messing with him.

"El Bomba is how I killed Britt Fairweather."

His eyebrows meet together in one single displeased line. "Now why would you say something like that? I find that in very poor taste."

"It's true," I cry. "I even tried to become a werewolf to, you know, make us even. To punish me. Torture me."

"Help me to understand here, your paper, 'Wolf Thoughts,' is that what you were trying to say with that?"

"No! That . . . that was a different wolf thing, that was poetry, *fiction*, but this, what I'm telling you now, *this* is reality." I'm not making sense. I'm panicky like I always get around him.

I catch him glancing at the clock, then he's up and leading me to the door. "I'm serious Augie. Anytime you want to talk. I mean *really* talk, not mess around, I'm here."

"Yes. Yes sir," I say as I am nudged into the cold hallway. He thinks I'm a wise guy. Or maybe a box of rocks. He needs to know I am not a box of rocks. That I did kill my best friend. That it haunts me. *Haunts me.* That I try, *really try* to do the right thing; with Britt, with my art projects. That I had other projects he might've liked better. I say, "I could still do my other idea to paint over the library building and principal's office!"

He looks at me with a nervous smile from the other side of the window. Then I hear the door lock click.

Alone in the hallway, the wolf scribbles in my hand, I can't move for several seconds. Then I walk out the exit, dumping my wolf pages in the trash by the door.

I place a photo on Cowboy Roy's nightstand.

He opens his eyes and rolls over in the hospital bed. "You got her good side," he says, studying the Polaroid of Ol' Paint.

"She's been getting a bucket of carrots every day," I say. "Oats too."

"How'd you do on your project?"

"Pass."

"There ya go. Any word on Nick?"

"Everyone's saying it's an immigration thing."

"Tell me another windy."

"Yeah, total cover-up."

"Them agents wanted to know what I know. I told them I was attacked by a werewolf and I got the bop on ma nut to prove it. They stood there laughing at me. Said that must've been some bop and did I believe in Dracula too? Acted like I was one sandwich short of a picnic." He takes a juice box sip. "I ain't saying another word to nobody. You don't neither, Aug."

A nurse stops in to check the screens that look like old-time Pong games. Roy perks up. "Nurse Velma, I ever sing ya 'Blood on the Saddle'?"

"Why, no," she says with a big smile as she waves bye-bye and leaves.

"Fillies," says Roy. "Hey Aug, looking forward to the first day of school?"

No.

I can't think of anything worse. I want to quit it all. Quit everything. But I force a smile and tell him, "Sure."

SIXTEEN

IT'S WHAT'S CALLED a fresh start. That's how Mom says I need to look at this new school year.

So I'm pedaling to school and it's light sweater weather with a chill in the air, but it's sunny too and I try to appreciate how good the sun feels on my face. There's a red cardinal pecking under Mr. Pennycross's feeder. Across the street Miss Dottie on her rider-mower squeezes in one last mow of the season. Leaves are turning. Autumn is coming. I watch yellow buses drop kids off in front of the school. The big announcement board greets us:

WELCOME BACK STUDENTS

No one has messed with it yet to say WELCOME BACK STUDS or anything. I try to take it all in: the flag waving in the breeze, the trimmed hedges, the freshly scrubbed steps and windows, the kids in brand-new back-to-school clothes with not-yet-used notebooks and unsharpened pencils. And I've almost convinced myself maybe this can be a fresh start when I hear the wolf howl. Not a real wolf howl, a kid making a wolf howl. I do a 360 but see nothing.

I hear it again. I move under a tree and bump into Juliana of all people.

I'm still trying to be upbeat so I say, "Greetings fair Cinderella," and I bow as if in Fairy Tale Place.

No answer. A glare.

“It’s me, Augie, from the park.”

“I know,” she says. “What am I, stupid?” She leans into my ear and whispers, “Why don’t you crawl back to your little brick house?”

She marches away. What was that all about? I head for the main building, then down the main hall where I hear, what? Another wolf howl?

At my locker someone puts me in a headlock from behind.

“Did you just pee here, Wolf Boy?” says the someone as my head gets forced down to a wet spot on the floor.

“What?” I say.

“This! What is this?”

“O-orange juice?”

It’s Hogg Wills. He pushes me into the lockers.

“Watch you don’t get wee-wee on you,” says his lackey, Tripp Vickles.

"I asked you a question, Wolf Boy." Hogg steps closer. "Did you mark your territory with your own wee?"

"No, I did not mark my territory."

"Owooooooooooooooooooo!" howls Vickles, the source of all the wolf howls.

A few students gather around.

"If you think it will prove anything," I say in my best fresh-start voice, "you can hit me but—"

He hits me in the chest so hard my rib cage rattles.

The bell rings and Mrs. Hawley rolls through the halls clapping her hands and shooing kids to their classes.

I stagger into the boys' room to splash my face with water and I'm staring at Hogg again. He kicks open a stall and pushes my head into a toilet bowl.

"Drink it, wolf!" he says.

"Dogs drink from toilets, not wolves," I say.

He takes my book bag, unzips it, and dumps the contents over the stall into the next toilet as a second bell rings. He pushes me a final time and storms off howling like a nitwit.

I stand and try to open the next stall. The door is locked. I knock.

The latch slides back and skinny Randall Weeks opens the door and hands me my books.

"Hogg?" he says, pulling my pencil from his hair.

I nod.

"Good thing I already had my pants down. Otherwise I woulda pooped myself." He zips up. "For what it's worth, I didn't think that stuff on Facebook was that bad."

"What stuff?"

"Your stuff. The wolf-talk stuff. The stuff every kid in school has been reading."

Throughout the day I notice kids whispering when I pass. I see someone point in my direction. At lunch I hide out in the library with my head behind a book. When the final bell rings I race home to read online what all the hullabaloo is about. Someone scanned my project pages. The ones I threw in the trash. Who knows who, who knows why. Kids do stuff like that. The jerk posted it all on Facebook with the heading: THIS "WOLF" THINKS HE IS BETTER THAN YOU. And that isn't even the worst of it. The worst part is some of the pages I don't even remember seeing before. When I turned that stuff in I was rushing. I grabbed every scribbly page from my book without checking too closely. If I *had* read everything in them, Tindall would've graded me on a robin collage instead of this craziness.

WOLF THOUGHTS

by AUGIE HOBBLE

runn runneen
runn runn
muss thinkstrate
losst alwaaz
Blak
moov
move Throo A dark

A few pages later is the part I don't remember.

stil Dark
canot see
so at leest dont see no
bullees aroun
no no hog

no hog who makes
funn of Others
because he has
Lo Self esteem.
beecaws he
smellz funni and lives in
a duble wide with brokin
windoes wich he feels
hehaz to make up for
with a bunch of meen stuf.
or Trip
who has no freinds but

Hogg.

no Kids who would rather pic on you than say a nise word to you. Kids Like joey Marks who hides his boogers under yorr desk in history class or Ott Killinger whoo steals other kids homework and writes his name on it. Or Jorge Tuna who makes fun of kids clothes even though his clothes look like hand me downs from a rodeo clown. There's no stuck up Juliana who never says boo to anyone their whole life. Never says kiss my foot or nothin. Or sneaks like Mindy Mudd who go on

Mr. Martin's computer when he leaves the room and peeks at private Facebook photos of his Booze Cruise to Jamaica then blames you. I am in the dark, yes. But Middle School is dark too. Middle School is not a place for nice guys. Middle School is not a place where a guy can get along simply by being a decent fellow. All a guy wants is to get by. To do his work. Have some friends. It should not be a place where if you are Darla Gumm and maybe embarrassed by a weird sore on your lip you have to watch people point and make fun of you.

Some might think what happened to

me is the worst thing that can happen

to a guy, but at least I am not

getting stuffed in ones own locker.

I am not getting teased.

I am not getting beat up which is a

whole lot better than a kick in the pants.

I am not getting kicked in the pants either.

That week at school was the longest week of my life.

It's been a while. A while since I've been to the fort. A while since I sat in this wobbly chair. A while since I've seen the glass owl, the Elmo curtains, and miniature Mona Lisa smiling her mysterious miniature Mona Lisa smile. I think of Mr. Fairweather and it makes me sad. I heard after Britt passed his hands shake so bad he can no longer make miniature portraits; and regular-size pictures, without that novelty of tininess, are just regular pictures. Who needs another regular-size Elvis for their living room? So rumor is when he returns from Tulsa he's going to work at the hardware store mixing paint.

I take my notebook from my book bag. This notebook that has caused me so much trouble. I take out the lighter I borrowed from Dad's drawer. I flip through my drawings and stories one last time. I flip past where the torn-out scribbly pages were.

And I do not believe what I see. New scribbles.

Return to Augie Hobble. I knew if I kept saying return to Augie Hobble that I would find a way to return to you. It's like in the Wizard of Oz when Dorothy keeps repeating "I want to go home, I want to go home," and she goes home. Willpower. For the longest time it seemed I was lost. Everyone here was going one way, heading toward the light, and I was heading back, going the other way. It was hard and it was dark but I knew I had to come back. Like I said, willpower, something I'm afraid you and your concentration issues would have a tough time with. In fact I hope there isn't a woodpecker outside the window now or you are distracted and not reading this very sentence.

With all due respect, Britt.

I don't know how long I was out but when I lift myself from the floor and reread the page a second time I notice 5:17 p.m. on my watch before I pass out again.

SEVENTEEN

5:23. Out for six minutes. I continue reading.

> *Augie, where are you? It's me.*
> *Why aren't you using this book anymore?*

I flip to the next page.

> *Augie, I think it's a week later.*
> *Where are you?*

Below that:

> *Augie, another day.*
> *Have you forgotten me?*
> *I am trying to reach you.*

I turn the page. It says:

> *Augie, I had to return. I had to come back.*

"Why?" I wonder out loud.

I watch as words write themselves on the blank page.

To tell you I forgive you.

"Britt!" I say. "Britt! Britt! You're back!" To the squirrels in the North Woods I must look as nutty as their squirrel poop, bawling like a baby and yelling at a book. I wipe at my tears and try to make a joke. "Did you bring me a present?"

Sorry Augie. I guess this is one vacation I can't bring you back a little something.

"But where are you?"

I don't know.

"Can you see anything around you?"

Yes. I see dead people.

"No!" I cry.

Yes. I am looking in a mirror. LOL.

"Stop kidding. Really, what's it like there?"

Fuzzy. Like I need glasses. But it gets better every day . . . well, there aren't really days here. Maybe I should say it gets clearer. Things get clearer all the time. And here I am, like a character from a ghost story with unfinished business. Augie, I had to tell you, don't feel so guilty about the cookie. I forgive you.

"I'm so, so sorry, Britt." Then after mulling it over for a second, I ask, "But really, wouldn't you think Spanish for peanut would be *peanuté*?"

No, cacahuate is peanut.

"Who would know that?"

Someone who once heard that peanuts can kill him? I knew all the names. You know, so I wouldn't die.

A list begins to write itself in the book.

Cacahuate is Spanish for peanut.
Aardnoot is Dutch for peanut.
Arachide is French for peanut.
Arachide is also Italian for peanut.
Erdnuss is German for peanut.

Jordnot is Swedish for peanut.
Ful Sudani is Arabic for peanut.

I close the book.

I open it a few minutes later. The list is still going.

Lo Huo Sheng is Chinese for peanut.
Amendoim is Portuguese for peanut.
Zemlianoi Orekh is Russian for peanut.
Rakkasei is Japanese for peanut.
Arachis hypogaea is Latin for peanut.

I tiptoe away from the book.

I'm just messing with you.

"Very funny."

No, I mean about your cookie.

"What? What are you saying?"

I'm saying do you actually think I'd eat a cookie from you? I gave it to a squirrel. With all due respect, you don't have the greatest track record when it comes to my allergies.

"But the paper said you died from peanuts."

I did. But not from your cookie. Did you know there are peanuts in French bread?

"No."

Because there are no peanuts in French bread. But French bread that has been baked on a tray that peanut butter brownies have also been baked on, that's another story.

"Are you kidding!?"

No, see the residue from the peanuts in the

"No, I mean are you kidding I've had to feel crummy all this time and I didn't even kill you?"

Don't sound so disappointed.

"So you came back to tell me? I don't know what to say Britt."

Someone had to tell you you didn't kill me. That would probably bug a guy.

"Why'd you draw that beheaded cat in my notebook?"

That wasn't a beheaded cat. I was sending you a sign. I tried to draw that stuffed toy you had from when you were little. Mr. Whiskers. You know, it's kinda hard to draw when you're trying to adjust to The Other Side. There's a certain amount of decompression that has to happen.

"Right. I could see that."

HEY! Now that we can communicate with each other this can be like our own secret club. We can call ourselves the Two Musketeers!

"What, they have muskets there?"

No. Musketeers don't have muskets anyway. They have swords.

"Then why are they called musketeers? Why aren't they called swordeers?"

You're missing the point.

"But really, why are they called musketeers?"

No idea.

"No idea? But now that you're supernatural, don't you have all the answers? You know, from *Beyond the Grave*?"

No. I still don't know how life or death works. I don't know how to spell Connettycut or know what's in Velveeta. I don't know why my parents like bluegrass music. I don't know where other dead people go. I don't even know where I went.

EIGHTEEN

I BIKE HOME like a madman, wind in my face, pedaling into a beautiful sunset and thinking of the Two Musketeers. Britt's back. It's magic. Like a fairy tale. Like a comic book.

I burst in the back door.

"Hi sweetie," says Mom. "Dinner in an hour."

"Smells great," I say.

"Well, it's meatloaf with broccoli. Sorry, not your favorite I know."

"I love meatloaf!" I say, bounding up to my bedroom.

I lock my door and plop down on my beanbag. I open my notebook to ask Britt if he's got meatloaf where he is when my balsa-and-tissue model airplane rolls down my desk and takes off, flying to the ceiling.

"Britt . . . ?"

I look to the book but instead of words appearing I hear Britt's voice in my head.

"Augie?" he says.

"How are you doing that?" I say.

"I concentrate and make it fly."

"No, how are you talking in my head?" My Polaroid camera floats off my desk and snaps a shot of the airplane before it does a loop-de-loop then crashes into my computer. "My plane! You broke it!"

"Sorry. Accident. But with all due respect, I'm kinda dead so I guess we're even."

Spammit! I know I will never again win an argument with Britt. He's got the ultimate comeback.

"I've been practicing," he says. "I'm learning how to do stuff. Watch."

I watch as my X-Men snow globe rises into the air and flies out the open window where I hear it roll down the roof to bust on the driveway.

"My snow globe!"

"Augie? Dead," he reminds me.

"Spammit!" Ultimate comeback. "Oh man, I just realized something. You can totally go in the girls' locker room."

"Oh, please," he says. Then his voice becomes almost like a whisper. "But I did float through my house a few minutes ago. I wandered the empty halls. My sister got my old figurines. She had them all out of order. Who puts a beefeater guard next to an Inuit? Completely different continents. The living room was kinda dusty. Mom's treadmill put away. Dad's paintbrushes all dried up . . ." His voice trails off.

Later in the bathroom I unbutton my pants and sit on the toilet.

"Britt?" I whisper.

Still later I am alone in the cellar looking for airplane glue.

"Britt?" I call.

At bedtime I lay my exhausted head on my pillow.

"Britt?"

"BOO!"

"Ah!" I scream.

"Gotcha!" says Britt.

"Okay, clearly we need to lay down some ground rules."

Next morning I can't wait to tell Claire about the miracle. I hop out of bed, skip breakfast, and run to the park. I reach her cart nearly out of breath. She is writing what looks like a grocery list. "Claire, you won't believe what happened," I say. She holds a finger in the air, silencing me as she finishes her list.

"Powerball's up to a hundred thirty million," she says. "I'm listing who gets what when I win." I'm about to bust.

Then without looking up she casually says, "Your friend Britt is back, right?"

Whoa, *what*? She really *does* see all.

Her face stretches into a big smile. She has tears in her eyes. "I had a vision of it last night!" She was just messing with me before. She can barely contain herself now. "I am so happy for you!" She gives me a hug. *A hug*. It feels nice.

"I told you there was something out of the ordinary to those scribbles," she says.

"The way I remember it you weren't so sure what they were."

"I said they were 'out of the ordinary.' That's pretty good."

"It doesn't matter now anyway. Don't need scribbles. I can hear him in my head."

"Really? That's way up there, paranormally speaking. Maybe there's a way to take it a step further, make him, you know, actually appear, materialize, dot, dot, dot."

"You could do that?"

"I've never tried but maybe. Let me think on it. Talk later?"

"Talk later."

I head off to polish the Old Lady Who Lives in a Shoe's shoe house. I turn back. "Isn't a clairvoyant playing the lottery cheating?"

"I don't actually play. I only pretend how I would share a jackpot. Most of my friends get a million."

"Am I on that list?"

"Don't know you that well yet."

I nod and take off.

"Hey," yells Claire, holding up the list. "What the heck, I'm putting you down for a million."

After our shifts we head for the North Woods. Claire said for her experiment she needed a place where Britt's vibrations would be strongest. A place not contaminated by too many other people. I suggested Fort Ninja.

We park our bikes and enter the fort.

"Pretty cool," she says.

"Not a bad crib," I say.

"Fantastic decorations. The owl is great and I love that little Mona Lisa."

"Thanks. I helped with a lot of that."

She blacks out the windows with paper. She says the darker the better. She clears off our wooden-crate table. She lays my notebook in the center of the table, lights a candle, and tells me to sit in the chair and concentrate on Britt.

"I'm more or less winging this," she says as she closes her eyes. She doesn't go into a trance or anything, but she looks pretty intense like she's fishing inside her head.

"Britt Fairweather. Can you hear me? Britt Fairweather we are trying to reach you on The Other Side. Are you picking up my voice Britt Fairweather?" she says. "Britt Fairweather do you have anything to tell us?"

"You let her in Fort Feng Shui?" Britt says in my head.

"He's here," I tell Claire.

"I don't hear him," she says.

Good, because Britt is being rude. Claire scrunches her face up and concentrates harder.

"So who is this girl? A girlfriend?" he says. "Why's her face all scrunched up like that? She looks constipated."

"Is he saying anything?" asks Claire.

"He says you look like you're concentrating."

"Britt Fairweather, we are attempting a materialization. I will attempt to transform your spirit vibrations to physical vibrations. I will attempt to make your physical presence known to us."

"Who ya gonna call? *Ghoooostbusters!"* sings Britt.

"Britt Fairweather . . . Britt Fairweather . . ." she chants. "Show us a sign."

Britt takes the BIGFOOT X-ING sign from the wall and floats it in front of her.

"A sign," he says.

"Ha, ha. Good one," I tell him in my head while snapping a shot.

She chants his name over and over, then lays her head on the table, exhausted.

"She dead?" asks Britt.

"She's only trying to help," I tell him to his face. "Holy Mother of Boo Berry!" I say out loud. "It worked. He's standing right here!"

"What? Where?" says Claire, lifting her head.

"Right here! Right in front of you!" I say, pointing at Britt plain as day. "It really worked!"

"I don't see him," she says. "He must materialize for you alone."

"Why?"

"I guess your connection is strongest."

As she says this he fades away.

"He's gone," I say.

"I must have a limited plan," says Britt in my head. "Gotta sign up for more minutes, har, har."

That night I call for Britt in my head but get no answer.

Next day Claire and I agree to meet again at Fort Ninja. But when we get there, there's no Fort Ninja.

I look left and right, but there's no sign of it.

"How do you make an entire fort disappear?"

"You don't," says Claire, looking up.

I follow her gaze up the tree to the fort. Only it's way better than our sorry little fort now. Now it's a spectacular tree house. I see why Britt didn't answer last night. He was busy.

"I went for a mid-century design. Split level," says Britt, materializing for me. "Pay careful attention to the green engineering. Notice how the limbs of the tree work seamlessly with, not against, the structure itself. Architecturally balanced, aesthetically pleasing to the eye." He puts on a haunted house voice. "Welcome foolish mortals to Tree House Feng Shui, heh, heh, heh."

"How did you . . . ?"

"I floated the pieces up. It was easy. I call it Caspering."

"As in Casper? The Friendly Ghost?"

"I'm not married to that name if you have a better one."

"Tell him this is amazing," says Claire, climbing the knotted rope.

"Hold it," I say, pulling out my camera. Britt and Claire pose on the balcony. CLICK.

I climb up, joining Britt and Claire.

"Look at us. Three Musketeers!" says Claire.

"*Two* Musketeers," says Britt. "Augie, tell her we're the Two Musketeers."

"Actually, Two Musketeers," I tell her. "Three Musketeers sounds silly."

"Whatever," says Claire.

NINETEEN

PEOPLE TEND TO beat a dead horse until another comes along. I endured a week of bullying thanks to that Facebook page, but the bullies sniffed out fresh meat in Randall Weeks. Because of a science kit he got for his birthday, he accidentally singed most of the hair off his head and eyebrows during a first attempt at Advanced Combustion. It was a lucky break for me. For a couple of days they called him Baldy and Cue Ball and Light Bulb. But once the bull has left the barn, as Cowboy Roy says, it ain't easy gettin' her back in. So when Randall's hair started sprouting again like a Chia Pet, the bullies got bored and circled back to me.

So I'm chaining my bike to the racks in front of Gerald R. Ford Middle School when Hogg Wills spots me.

"Hobble," he yells, tossing a softball into the air. "Wanna fetch?"

“I told you before, you’re confusing your dogs and wolves,” I say.

He dances around, waving the ball. “Come get the ball. Here boy. That’s a goo’ boy. Nice doggie. Augie doggie. Get the ball, boy.”

A crowd gathers. I see Juliana. She’s laughing with the rest.

“Are you going to fetch or am I going to have to spank you with a rolled-up newspaper?” Hogg says.

I look him square in the eye. “Guess I better fetch,” I say.

But I don’t budge. I only hold out my hand. Then watch as the ball pries itself from Hogg’s hand to float over kids’ heads before landing in my hand. The kids can’t believe it. Hogg can’t believe it. He walks to me, feeling the air in front of him for trick wires. He snatches the ball back.

I can’t resist saying it. “Goo’ boy!” I shouldn’t have. It was mean and there’s no need to reinforce the stereotype that bullies make other bullies.

Plus it really pees him off.

His eyes narrow to slits. His neck turns blood red. He rears back to punch me but a book breaks free from Juliana's arms, blocking his swing. "Owwwww!" he screams, his fist smashing into the book.

The crowd is pretty substantial now and they cheer. Hogg, confused, bewildered, steps back.

"What's going on?" he says.

"We done?" I say.

"*No, we're not done!* I'm not buying this," he says. "Do something else. Make that lunch pail fly into the tree."

"That all? Child's play."

I turn to Jorge Tuna's Hobbit lunch pail. "You might call this a light lunch," I joke to my growing audience. I point at the lunch pail.

Nothing happens.

I point again. Nothing.

Hogg smiles and stomps toward me. He is about to deck me when the lunch pail whooshes up into the tree. The crowd gasps. I hop up on a bench. I notice the mural on the science building behind me. It's of the solar system and I am directly in front of the big painted moon. I throw my head back and howl, "Owwwwoooooooooo!"

The crowd laughs and applauds as the bell rings. Everyone heads for class, leaving Hogg behind to once more search the air for hidden wires.

I call to Jorge before he gets to the main entrance. He turns as his lunch pail flies back into his hands.

Several kids slap me on the back. A few actually congratulate me on "my" Facebook page. "You only told what everyone was thinking," says Ray-Z, coolest kid in school, speaking to me for the first time ever.

"True that," I say.

"Did you see that little R.I.P. shrine to me?" says Britt, materializing.

"So that's where you were." A bunch of kids made a shrine to Britt with his picture framed in school-color ribbons and plastic flowers. "You left me hanging! I thought Hogg was going to throw *me* in that tree."

"Did you see the photo they chose? It was from like two years ago. I had the missing front tooth. Total nerd. They couldn't have used the cool one of me with the light saber?"

"Forget about the shrine, Britt. We just had ourselves a Hogg roast!" We do a little dance on the steps of the school.

To anyone watching it would have looked like me doing a nerdy happy dance by myself. But no one's going to tease me about it. Not today.

I look back at Hogg. He's looking all around the tree. I actually feel a little sorry for the guy. A little.

Mr. Fields stands before a map of the United States. He opens his desk drawer and produces a jar of pushpins. He removes the lid. He hand gestures over the pins like a game show model. Mr. Fields does stuff like this all the time. He points to things without talking and we're supposed to know what the heck he means. He writes on the whiteboard STATE CAPITALS. He gestures to the map then gestures back to the pins. Map, pins. He wants us to put the pins in the capitals. I think. He sort of dances between the desks, then stops at mine. He gestures from me to the map. Me, map. I stand. I walk to the jar and take out a pin. I move to the map. Unlike most maps, this one doesn't have the capitals highlighted. I see New York. I of course put the pin in New York City.

"WRONG!" yells Mr. Fields, breaking character. "Albany! Albany is the capital of New York."

He turns his back on me and addresses the class. "I want each of you to choose a pin and put it in a state. And if anyone else is incorrect, there will be a test on state capitals for the entire class."

Capital punishment.

Mr. Fields returns to his elegant mime character. He smiles, tips an invisible hat to the class, and turns back to me. And sees the map now filled with fifty pushpins in all their correct capitals.

Britt's good with capitals.

Mr. Fields looks at me. He looks at the map. Me, map, me, map. I tip an invisible hat and return to my seat.

Science class. We've all brought potatoes from home. We're going to make potato lamps. I know this experiment from fifth grade, so I have it down pretty good. You wrap one end of electrical wire around a penny and the other end around a galvanized nail. You cut a potato in half and stick the penny in. In the other half you stick the nail. You take two alligator clips, attach them to the wire, and attach the opposite ends to a small LED light. It lights up. Electric charge. Pretty cool.

But today I have something else in mind. Britt. He's in my mind. We have a quick chat.

I explain to Ms. Newton that my uncle Jubal is an amazing farmer and that he grew my "magic potato."

I see Britt in position at the classroom light switch. When I fire my potato up, Britt flips the lights off and on and off and on and off and on. It's like a lightning storm. The class goes crazy. All except Randall Weeks. He's still a bit shell-shocked from science experiments. He covers his Chia Pet head.

Coach Barbolak marches in front of our bench, jutting his thumb at victims. "Verna, third base. Demos, left field. Lee, catcher. Edmond, second base. T.B., center. Snow, pitcher. Hobble, right field." I grab my mitt and hustle to my position.

"We ready?" I say to Britt in my head.

"Ready. Hey batta batta . . ."

A pop fly.

I race to position myself beneath it. I hold out my glove. It's heading right for me! I'm gonna catch it! Then BONK, it's like it hit a glass wall. The ball falls to the ground. Britt! I go to pick it up but it rolls quickly away from me. Britt must've flubbed it and now accidentally kicked it.

"Hobble!" yells Coach Barbolak. "Get it together!"

I pick up the ball and throw it over the second baseman's head. Great.

"Sorry, Augie," says Britt.

"Yeah, what happened?"

"I may be supernatural but I still super-suck at baseball."

"So when Jack London's Grey Cub says: 'Life lived on life. There were the eaters and the eaten . . . ,' what do you think he was getting at?" asks Ms. Sanford, looking up from her copy of *White Fang*.

"Just that," I say before I can stop myself.

"Augie?" says Ms. Sanford.

"I mean, with all due respect, it's not symbolic or anything. Eat or be eaten. It's the law of the wolf."

"Well, that's one way to—"

I surprise even myself when I step in front of my English class and assume a wolflike crouch. "You see, the food chain is one of many tiers. But at the top, that's always going to be *Canis lupus*." I extend my hand to the Beanie Critters on Ms. Sanford's desk and Britt floats her Beanie squirrel, Beanie mouse, and Beanie owl up my arm. I fake juggle as Britt twirls them in a circle and I recite lines memorized from my old wolf wall. "With no natural enemies to speak of, *Canis lupus* keeps the population in check by preying on the weak. His massive rear molars crush bones like nuts in a nutcracker though *Canis lupus* does little actual chewing. He might feast on several prey at a single feeding. Like so." I open my mouth and let each stuffed animal drop behind me as I fake swallow them. I notice Hogg Wills in the back of the class looking uncomfortable. "And that," I say, "is the law of the wolf."

I return to my desk.

"That's, um, a very informative answer, Augie," says Ms. Sanford.

"Nice job floating those Beanie Critters," I say to Britt after class.

"Caspering."

"Weren't you going to come up with a better name?"

"I could call it Marleying."

"Huh?"

"Marley's Ghost. *A Christmas Carol*?"

"Huh?"

"We can be Marley and Me."

"Huh?"

"Forget it."

The final bell rings and I exit the front door. A bunch of kids walk beside me.

"Hey Hobble, how's it going?"

"Hi Augie. Nice going in English."

We round the corner and come upon Hogg Wills and Tripp Vickles. They're stomping on Jorge Tuna's Hobbit lunch pail. They see me and stop midstomp.

"We weren't doing anything," says Hogg innocently.

"We didn't know you were here," says Tripp.

I don't say a word. Kinda impolite to make them squirm though. "You can go now," I say.

They do. They run.

Students cheer.

Jorge cheers.

Juliana appears before me. "Hail to your grace," she says with a royal bow.

"Thanks Juliana," I say, then excuse myself when I see Claire waiting at the bike rack.

"Hey," I say.

"Hey," says Claire. "Thought I'd walk you home."

She does. Along with about ten extra kids from school. They just want to follow.

Some ask about what they saw today. I say it was only magic tricks and a magician never reveals his secrets. Inside though I am on cloud nine remembering the greatest day of my life.

TWENTY

OCTOBER THIRTY-FIRST. Big movie lights called Kliegs send ghostly beams into the Halloween night. Guests arrive by the hundreds, curious to see if Scary Tale Place will scare at all. The local paper is covering the grand opening. TV-3 too. All enter beneath the black and orange main gate to eerie wind, screams, and bubbling cauldron sound

effects. To the right is Humpty Dumpty's wall where two legs dangle bodiless. No one fixed Humpty after Nick and Ol' Paint smashed him to bits, so all that was needed was a little fake blood on his cement stumps. To the left, Shriek the Blue Ogre and the Old Lady from the Shoe lob sockfuls of candy "corn" to guests. The Old Lady moans about the horrific corns the big shoe gave her feet. "Take them, take them," she wails. Fort Fortitude has become Fort of Fear with skeletons dangling on hangman ropes from the look-out tower, while an executioner beckons guests to join the hanging party.

It isn't the Night Before Christmas. Still, lots of *creatures are stirring* at the North Pole. Not the Frankenstein monster though. He's in Santa's bed *resting his brain for a long winter's nap*. It's in a big jar on the nightstand.

Over at Birthday Town, renamed Deathday Town, guests can fill out their own death certificate and snap a picture with the undertaker. And at Storybook Village we figured

if it's already broke, don't fix it. We added a few cobwebs and plastic spiders to the rundown, dilapidated buildings but other than that it needed nothing else.

Dad checks the main gate tallies twice and still can't believe it: 2,100 guests.

The first of the fireworks explode. Yes, tonight we have the pyrotechnics and the live music and the free pop (while supplies last). This is big.

"Augie," calls Claire from her cart. I sweep over to her. "I think something bad's going to happen tonight."

A series of spiderlike fireworks explode, ashes floating down to the guests like black snowflakes. "Something with the fireworks?" I ask.

"I don't know yet."

"Ungh! You're always doing that. It's so frustrating."

A fiery orange pumpkin-shaped firework bursts overhead.

"Well, keep working on it," I tell her as I head for Fort of Fear.

I hear power chords coming from Stage Fright (formerly Wilderness Stage). I am surprised to see Moze with a guitar. There are two other guys on bass and drums too. Oh man, it's the Route 666 kid and his friend with the wimpy chin-whiskers. They're all wearing T-shirts that say THE EFFLUVIUMZ. They turn the amps up as loud as they'll go as they thrash at their instruments. Then, when it feels as if it couldn't get any louder, I hear a sound not unlike asthmatic cats. It's Darla Gumm and her accordian! I think they are playing "Monster Mash," but to be honest it's hard to tell.

I hear someone yelling behind me. I cup my ear. "What?"

"I *said*," yells Dad, "what do you think?"

"Great Dad. Really. Everything. Congratulations."

Darla hits a sour note. We wince.

"Well, almost everything. I had to cut some corners on the music budget," says Dad.

The Effluviumz finish with a wall of feedback and Moze dancing all herky-jerky like a zombie.

He sees me and gives me the devil horns salute with his fingers. I give him a thumbs up and point to his Effluviumz shirt. He comes to the edge of the stage. "Thanks for the name, nerd. Except you were wrong. Effluvium isn't a killer virus. It's the stuff they pump out of septic tanks." He turns and shows me the back of his T-shirt, a graphic of a toilet bowl. "Which, by the way, is way cooler."

"BravO," says Dad patting me on the back and walking away.

Claire comes running to me. "I know what the bad thing is."

"Me too. 'Monster Mash.' It was horrible."

"No," says Claire. "Something else. Something at the main gate."

We get to the main gate box office and knock. No response.

"Kick it in," says Claire.

"What?"

"Now!" she says.

I kick the door. I practically break my foot. The door doesn't budge.

Hovering over the ticket office is a statue of Paul Bunyan. I borrow his giant ax and force the door open. Tied up on the floor, elderly cashier Ruby Mae looks up with pleading eyes.

"Ruby, who did this?"

"Mmmm mm mm," she says.

"Remove the gag first," says Claire, rolling her eyes.

I remove the gag.

"Big Bad Wolf," Ruby Mae says. "Moze. He got the cashbox."

"No, Moze was at Stage Fright," I tell her.

"Well that suit wasn't walkin' by its lonesome."

We untie her and she calls Dad. I grab a flashlight and we begin searching the park.

We search attractions and huts. We meet up with Security.

“Let’s fan out,” says Security Head Sandy. “If you see something, use a park phone to call. Don’t try to be a hero.”

“No problem, there,” says Claire.

We fan out. Claire heads to the North Pole, Security combs the parking lot. I hit Storybook Village, which due to its lazy decorating is practically guest free. My flashlight beam combs every surface like a searchlight in a prison break movie.

I see a shadow moving in and out of the storybook huts.

I follow.

I check Geppetto’s Shop. I check Shriek’s Cottage. I open the door to Grandma’s House. I scan the room with my flashlight. The beam passes over the statue of Red Riding Hood. I scan the curtains and closets and pause on the wolf sleeping in Grandma’s bed. I move closer. I shine the light in his cartoon eyes. No movement. It’s the stuffed dummy that’s always there. I turn to leave and my flashlight shines on the Big Bad Wolf hiding behind the door.

He pushes me against the wall and tries to flee, but I trip him. He falls against the plastic PLAY ME button. The attraction narration begins:

Once upon a time there was a dear little girl who was loved by everyone, but most of all by her grandmother . . .

He takes a swing at me, I duck, and he knocks the picnic basket from Red Riding Hood. It lands on the floor along with Red's plaster arm. Plastic apples and bread rolls roll every which way. He exits. I run after him but stumble on Red's arm and slam into the doorjamb. I fall back and the room goes fuzzy for a second. I come to with the wolf standing over me. "You okay?" he says. I'm okay. He nods and goes, "Weeeell . . ." and turns to leave.

"Jim?" I say.

He stops.

"Jim, that you?"

"Now what'd you go and do that for?"

It's Jim. The sweeper who's always having me clean up his messes. He rips the sash from Grandma's curtain and binds my hands behind my back.

"Why, Jim?" I ask.

"The cashbox?" He makes a kinda "why not?" shrug.

He removes his head to better see his knot tying.

"I knew it was you from the way you said 'Wellllll.'"

"Give the guest a prize." He shoves a plastic apple in my mouth. He wraps a gag around it. "Growing up, my daddy... whenever he was through with a conversation he'd go *well* and get up and leave. He gave the word two syllables, *way-yell*. You'd be telling him about your day at school and he'd go *waaaay-yell* and your story was over. Didn't give two spits if you made the football team. Didn't give two spits if you got a B+ on your paper on the care and feeding of the horny toad. He'd go *waaaaay-yell* and mister, you were done. The end." He jerks me up by my elbows. "So Augie." He puts his head back on. *"Waaaaaay-yeeeeellll . . ."* he says. "We're done."

He peeks from the door left and right, then pushes me out in front of him.

He doesn't get two steps before a big oversize Paul Bunyan ax comes flying at him from the woods, slicing through the air and hitting him square on the neck and lopping off his wolf head. The severed head bounces on the ground, coming to a stop at my feet. It stares up at me with painted eyes. The headless body continues on, running in circles. It's like one of Aunt Mavis's chickens running with its head cut off. I think I am going to be sick.

But no, Jim has not been beheaded. In a moment his sweaty face rises slowly, cautiously, from the neck hole of the oversize costume body.

"You see that!? Haunted, man. Haunted," Jim says.

Britt unties me and I spit out the apple.

"Cashbox," I demand.

"Ain't got it," he says.

WHOOSH. Invisible Britt swings the ax over his head.

"I hid it. I swear."

From Grandma's House the recorded narration is still going: *It occurred to the hunter that the wolf might have devoured the grandmother, so he cut open its stomach and . . .*

Britt holds Jim's arms behind him. I unzip the costume zipper all the way down his belly until the cashbox spills out.

Security Cam 01

Security Cam 02

In a minute Security arrives.

In another minute, Dad and Hank in a golf cart followed by Claire.

In another minute, TV-3.

I hand Dad the cashbox. He opens it. It's all there.

"Bravo," he says weakly.

Security cuffs Jim. TV-3 asks for a comment but all he says is, "Haunted, haunted, haunted," over and over.

TWENTY-ONE

BRITT'S MOM AND DAD sit in their living room. Back from Tulsa. It never really sunk in before how different their house is from ours. They have collectibles. Lots of collectibles. One bookcase alone is filled with glass owls. The guest bathroom has a cushioned toilet seat. There's a large painting over the couch of a cottage in the woods, the soft glow of candlelight in all its windows. It's lit by a kind of desk lamp growing from the top of the gold frame. Miniature paintings in miniature frames are displayed in unexpected nooks and corners. There's one on the mantel. It's of Britt. I've seen it before but now it's got little half-scale black ribbons on either side of it.

"How are you holding up, Augie?" says Mrs. Fairweather. "Ted, mute that."

Mr. Fairweather has a tennis game on, but he isn't even looking at the TV. He's kind of looking off at nothing. Mrs. Fairweather takes the remote and turns it off. "Augie?"

"I'm well," I say, remembering to say the proper "well" instead of "good." "How . . . how are you?"

"We have Britt's little sister to keep us busy. She's a handful." Mrs. Fairweather laughs but not really. At knee level on a coffee table, a plate of cookies. "Have one," she says.

I stare at them, remembering El Bomba.

"No thank you," I say.

"You had something to tell us?"

I feel an elbow dig into my side. It's Britt prodding me. I unzip my book bag. I remove the glass owl and put it on the coffee table.

"My owl. You found it. I was so disappointed in Britt."

Another elbow dig.

"It wasn't Britt. *I* took it. For our fort. I'm sorry."

"No, keep it," she says, catching a tear with her little finger. "*I'm* sorry."

"But it's part of your collection."

Mr. Fairweather puts an arm around his wife. "Keep it," he says.

"He was a good boy," she says.

"Mrs. Fairweather, Mr. Fairweather, I want you to know Britt is . . ." But before I can say anything, Britt forces me up and toward the door.

"I know," says Mrs. Fairweather. "It's like he's still with us in a way. Isn't it?"

"Yes," I say as Britt pushes me out. "Yes, it is."

When we reach the sidewalk between our houses I say, "You owe me one."

"I know," he says.

"Britt, we should tell them," I say.

"One day," says Britt. "Not today."

ONCE THERE WAS A GUY NAMED AUGIE HOBBLE.

FOR A WHILE THIS GUY AUGIE WAS GETTING A LOT OF FLAK FROM BULLIES AND SUCH. HE THOUGHT HE WANTED TO BECOME A SUPER WOLF AND FIGHT THEM ALL.

THEN HE THOUGHT HE KILLED HIS BEST FRIEND WITH A COOKIE SO HE WANTED TO BECOME A WOLF-BEAST TORTURED FOR ALL TIME.

BACK THEN HE WANTED TO BE ANYTHING BUT HIMSELF.

NOW ALL HE WANTS TO BE IS AUGIE HOBBLE.
HIS PROSPECTS LOOK GOOD. HE'S BACK TO TAKING PICTURES AND DRAWING COMICS AND WRITING STORIES.

MOST OF THE PAST YEAR SEEMS LIKE A DREAM.
A VERY MESSED-UP DREAM.
EXCEPT FOR SOME THINGS, *YOU KNOW*, DOT, DOT, DOT . . .

OH YEAH, HE HAS A NEW JOB TOO.
ONE OF THE HOSTS GOT A FULL-TIME GIG PLAYING ROCK AND ROLL AT THE BOWLING ALLEY, SO THERE WAS A POSITION OPEN AT THE PARK . . .

MEET THE NEW BIG BAD WOLF.

I walk with Claire as the sun sets behind the crooked rooftops of Fairy Tale Place. Atop a twelve-foot cement cake, "Happy Birthday to You" plays through the static of a tinny speaker. Claire joins in. I start to hum something else, *any-thing else* so I don't have the tune in my head all night. But I'm saved when the prerecorded music crackles, pops, and goes out halfway through the song.

"Crummy old park," I say.

"It's not crummy," says Claire. "It's strange. And cool. I came here as a kid. I loved it then, I still love it."

We stop at a freshly painted sign:

COMING THIS CHRISTMAS. MERRY TALE PLACE

In my head I hear, "Bet you a buck your Dad swaps out that cashbox for a heavy-duty safe."

"Bet you a buck you're right," I say.

"Is he following us?" says Claire.

"Oops, did I answer him out loud?" I say.

"My shift is starting anyway. Gotta get to Wardrobe," she says. "Later, Three Musketeers."

"Two Musketeers!" hollers Britt in my head.

“She can’t hear you,” I tell him, watching her go. “Ow.”

Then I hear another voice.

“Hobble!” Walking toward me is Special Special Agent Edwards.

“Back to prick another one of my fingers?”

“Naw, no more tests.” He eyes me up and down. “Though if I *were* giving a fashion exam you might get a D- for those sneakers . . .” This coming from the guy with the socks and sandals.

“Came by to tell you I finally found one of them carved coyotes. Your mom was right. Santa Fe. Who would’ve guessed?”

“Who *is* this guy?” says Britt in my head.

“Trouble,” I answer.

“So Hobble,” he says, “when I was driving you home few weeks back you mentioned a previous wolf attack.”

“Right. Boy who cried werewolf I think you called me.”

“Aw, I was just funnin’ around with that,” he says, poking me in the arm. “But hey, no kidding, you never mentioned if there was anyone else there at that previous encounter.”

“Why do you ask?”

"No reason. Just being thorough."

"Well it was just me. Me, the Big Bad Wolf and Little Red Riding Hood."

"Ha!" he says, jutting his hand out. "I'll be saying adios, then. For good."

I shake his hand. "For good?"

"HQ's transferring me down south, Meh-Hee-Co way."

"Chasing chupacabra?"

He smiles. "I have no idea what that is."

"Mexican Bigfoot," says Britt in my head.

"He knows," I tell Britt.

"Hasta la vista," Edwards says, turning those socks and sandals toward the the main exit.

"That was the agent you told me about," says Britt.

"Yep."

"You didn't tell him about Hoodie that night."

"Nope. Have him questioning me the rest of my life? No thanks."

"Of course he could have just asked him himself," says Britt.

"Asked who?"

"Over there. In the shade."

I look to the shade. A guest creeps through the shadows weaving in and out of bushes, a trail of corn dog wrappers dropping behind him.

I move closer, picking up the wrappers. The guest steps into the light. I see his red hood.

He's got that hoodie pulled tight around his head but I can still make out a shadowy face covered in long, coarse hairs. He points to the foil wrappers in my hand and through sharp white teeth and shiny black lips says, "How's business? Picking up?"

He pushes past, giggling at his joke. He pulls his hoodie strings tighter as he trots in the direction of Edwards.

I just stand there watching him. Frozen. Then Britt's voice brings me back to reality.

"Picking up," he says. "I get it."

The twinkle lights of Fairy Tale Place begin popping on, one building at a time all down Lilliput Lane and up to the North Pole.

"We live in a weird, weird world," I say.

From Birthday Town, a tinny speaker comes back to life.

"Well, Claire is right about one thing," Britt says. "This place *is* strange."

"And cool," I say.

Then together we sing that birthday song even after the music crackles, pops, and goes out again.